ERRATA EDITION 3/1

THANKS FO[R]
CITY BOOKS!

MAY YOU TRULY LIVE
RIGHT UP TO THE MOMENT
YOU TRULY DON'T.

ALL THE BEST

Also by Chris Rodell

"Use All The Crayons! The Colorful Guide
to Simple Human Happiness," 2014

Chris blogs near daily at
www.EightDaysToAmish.com

THE LAST BABY BOOMER

BOOMER

The Story of the
Ultimate Ghoul Pool

CHRIS RODELL

THE LAST BABY BOOMER
THE STORY OF THE ULTIMATE GHOUL POOL

Cover concept & design by Robyn John
Author photo by Brian F. Henry

iUniverse books may be ordered through booksellers or by contacting:

iUniverse
1663 Liberty Drive
Bloomington, IN 47403
www.iuniverse.com
1-800-Authors (1-800-288-4677)

ISBN: 978-1-4917-8500-3 (sc)
ISBN: 978-1-4917-8501-0 (e)

Library of Congress Control Number: 2015920295

Print information available on the last page.

iUniverse rev. date: 12/22/2015

To those who encourage the discouraged — the ones who persevere despite the rejections, the reaction, the results, the sleepless nights and the nagging voices, both within and without, advising you to come to your senses and just give up — this book is with love dedicated.

That means YOU, Allan Zullo. Thanks!

This book is self-published by the author. That means it enjoys none of the traditional benefits provided by deep-pocket publishing houses. It has no marketing budget so if you find it entertaining, please tell others. No crackerjack teams of plot doctors suggested improvements in story progression, character development or point of view. What follows is wholly organic. And while the author has painstakingly labored to eliminate every typo, grammatical error and sloppily constructed sentence, he realizes he has inevitably failed. The following pages contain those literary scourges and for that the author is sorry. He hopes you won't hold it against him and will, in fact, notify him at storyteller@chrisrodell.com so he can correct future editions. He thanks you in advance for your forbearance and believes you share his understanding that mistakes in life and literature are unavoidable. Like most of you, he believes to err is humon.

AUGUST 2083

The line to behold the dying man throbbed and pulsed within 5,000 feet of velvet rope. The crimson tethers were like arteries rushing blood to the center of a sick heart. They stretched down the marbled hall past the restrooms clear back to where they'd hung the crappy Andy Warhol. The ceaseless multitudes bore the pained expressions of hens consumed with thoughts of trying to lay square eggs. They clutched their $25 tickets and rubbed their good luck charms with urgent impatience. The doomed man's chain-smoking primary care physician hadn't scanned a single chart or much less bothered to visit his patient in more than 18 months and remained dogged in his shrill conviction that the patient, Martin Jacob McCrae, would drop dead any second.

That's when all the real fun would begin.

Nurse Becky Dudash knew just what she'd do when he died. She'd use her fresh millions to insulate herself from a humanity she'd grown to loath. For the past three years, her every dream was of the old man's demise, a death she was by Congressional fiat restricted from either preventing or hastening. She loved him with her whole heart and found it odd how often she dreamed of taking a pillow and laughing

1

maniacally as she pressed it down without pity over the once-handsome face that had begun to look to her like it had been whittled from a giant meatball. But his was legislatively ordained to be a natural death no matter how much a moral quagmire his endless life was proving to be.

McCrae lay motionless in the room across the hall from the nurse's station with its glowing security monitors, the stacks of take-out menus, and not a single thermometer, stethoscope, syringe or item that resembled even the most basic nursing equipment. At the foot of his bed standing directly on top of a big black "X" was the latest contestant who, like millions who'd stood there before him, was saying quiet, earnest prayers the all-loving God would take this used up old relic and hustle his bony little ass to whatever heaven or hell awaited men like him. "Please, God, I need the money," begged the thrice-divorced 53-year-old trucker from Louisville. "I'll use most of it to help the poor. I promise. Please … I've got just four minutes left! C'mon, Lord! Hurry!"

A rumpled easy chair in a darkened corner had been engaged in a stalemate staring contest with McCrae's hospital bed for nearly five years. The once-grand chair had become an upholstered host organism to a parasitic slouch named Buster Dingus. To the right of Dingus was the lever he'd robotically tug in exactly — tick, tick, tick — 3 minutes and 56 seconds. Had anyone bothered to gaze upon him — no one ever did — they would have seen a wan face numb with sleepless fatigue. His stare never drifted from a large screen wall-mounted television. His jaws ceaselessly worked an ever-present gum wad whose spearmint flavor had long since vamoosed. The constant chewing accentuated temples so pronounced that every chomp seemed to turn his face peanut shaped. Buster was maybe the only person on the planet with a vested interest in hoping that McCrae's death was distant. He knew what he going to do the instant the old man died, he hoped, many oppressive years from now.

But when it finally came — and almost everyone believed it was bound to come — he was going to reach into the right hip pocket of his garish purple uniform and pull out the antique cigarette lighter he'd stolen from his grandfather when Buster was just a boy. He'd cross the white linoleum to the balcony of the white room where the 105-pound white man had lay dying for years. He'd slide open the glass doors and reach across to the platform where the box marked, "DANGER. EXPLOSIVES. FIREWORKS." stood. After nearly a dozen or so thumb tickling flicks, flame would be lowered to fuse and the 50-pound pyrotechnic would be on its way. And as the throng 47 floors below gazed up in wonderment and anticipation at the expanding starburst in the sky, Buster was planning on finally spitting out his gum and hoping it hit a deserving face staring — cross your fingers — gape-mouthed toward the heavens.

The world's last baby boomer would be dead. The day-long parades would commence within scant hours.

But until then, monotony would reign as long as the endless line of men and women who had come from around the solar system to pray for the death of Marty McCrae kept surging through the etched glass double doors with the ceaseless regularity of the eternal tides. Buster had spent nearly five straight years seated in the small room with the speechless McCrae, a former couch potato who had graduated to a persistent vegetative state. In that time,

Buster had never said a single word in the direction of McCrae. And whether it was out of contempt or simply a reflex function of a comatose body, the only sound McCrae had ever made in the direction of Dingus was produced by the gentle trumpet of uncontrollable flatulence.

Not that Buster was insulted. The prehistoric old man was his meal ticket and Buster felt an abiding affection for anyone who had buttered his bread as deeply and evenly as McCrae buttered his. People were paying Buster $25 a pop to step into the room with McCrae for precisely 14 minutes and 59.5 seconds. The line that had slammed into formation in 2078 had run without break, day and night, for five consecutive years. From his easy chair, Buster was witness to tales of epic poignancy and pathos. He'd heard prayers in so many foreign tongues that he figured he could now bluff his way through supper table grace in more than a dozen different languages. Some would have been moved to pen poems and epic odes to the sweeping majesty of human desperation. Buster just watched television and kept counting the money.

When the clock ticked down to near double zero, a prerecorded phone sex voice would gush, "Your time's up! Better luck next time! You can play all day, any day, so come back soon!"

This was followed by a businesslike male voice speaking at auctioneer speed: "ThisCourtesyMessageWasBroughtToYouByTheMakersOfCoca-Cola,NowAvailableonKeplers-22bThroughf," and the slight, crisp *ding!* of a wall-mounted bell.

That's when Buster would non-nonchalantly reach to his right for the 3-foot lever and give it a short tug. The trapdoor could be set on automatic, but Dingus enjoyed a quick burst of adrenaline every time he gave the creaky lever a yank. The action would trigger a spring releasing the large trap door beneath the X, thus voiding the dreams, not to mention the presence of the dreamer standing upon it. Down they'd go. Before the echo of the falling screams had fully faded, the exterior doors would open and a conveyor belt would deposit the next contestant on the X a split second after it'd slammed shut. The clock would reset and the prayers that were being routinely ignored by both Buster and other beseeched deities would begin anew.

It had been this way for 18 months since the old man fell from consciousness and this is the way it would be until the old man was finally, mercifully, declared dead. Rain or shine, night or day, they lined up no fewer than 400 deep and took their chances. Even today, with angry lightning approaching Manhattan from the southwest, a throng waited patiently on the sidewalk to purchase tickets in hopes they'd be the lucky one who got to watch McCrae breathe his last.

Buster relied on McCrae the way worms did dirt. Like McCrae, Buster hadn't set foot outside of the suite for five years, way back in 2078. He would not leave until McCrae's demise, something the old man, too, had been endlessly eager to achieve. Buster remembered his ceaseless complaints. "Nobody should have to live this long," McCrae'd often moan back when he was still fully capable of speech and rational thought. Still, McCrae'd been enjoying the attention, the pampering and the fragrant nearness of

5

the luscious Nurse Dudash. Her eyes were the color of Elvis Presley's turquoise belt buckle and Marty thought she was sweet enough to cause cancer in lab rats.

But then came the collapse in March 2081. McCrae was talking for days about nothing but humbug, humbug, humbug, and how Charles Dickens had stolen it from the rest of the year and saddled it upon Christmas.

"It's a perfectly good year-round word," he said in between spoonfuls of marshmallow-studded cereal. "True humbug can happen any time of year. It happened in Oz, smack dab in the middle of the Emerald City. Really, humbug has nothing to do with Christmas. In America, humbug can always find a home."

But no one listened or cared, especially the prim, impatient, preternaturally mature and pony-tailed Girl Scout from Jakarta who was rushing through a list of prepared questions that would earn her the coveted Girl Scout Gold Award. She was efficient. She was intense. She was business-like. She was mature. Diwata Bautista was everything McCrae had never been so he capriciously decided to begin making up ridiculous answers to her serious questions about the past 117 years. If she didn't care about humbug he might as well inflict some of it on her, right there in the middle of March.

A coquettish brunette, Marty sensed Diwata would have been pretty had she smiled. But the only time she'd smile was for the two seconds it'd take to pose for a new profile picture, which she updated on an hourly basis.

He could tell she was really taking care of business when she dispensed with the selfie right away and plunged right into her scripted questions with crisp efficiency.

"Do you remember the moon landing?"

"Yes, I was just a boy, but I clearly remember the fuss my father made. Little did he know then that nearly sixth years later his son would help make the Sea of Tranquility like a lunar Myrtle Beach. Tell me, have you ever enjoyed a round of moon golf? It's, indeed, a soulful diversion."

"No. Golf's boring," Diwata said. "And please don't distract me with any more of your questions. Time's short. Do you remember the Kennedy assassination?"

"No. I was still in the womb. My mother carried me for ten months and three weeks. Quite a long time. If things would have worked out the way I wanted, I'd still be there today. It was quite pleasant and I loved my mommy. That's why I always took long, warm baths throughout my life. It was the nearest I could get to being back in the womb without inconveniencing Mom."

"Do you remember being on board the Titanic?"

"You mean the blockbuster movie set? Oh, sure. I was earning $250 a day for three weeks until they fired me for blowing the whistle about the drowned extra. Nobody believed me until I threatened to go to the TV stations. But at that point, they weren't going to let the death of one lousy extra stop the filming of a $200 million mega-hit. They offered me a cool $500,000 to keep my mouth shut. I was never one to let principle stand in the way of a nice payday. But I held out until they agreed to let me be in an underwater scene with Kate Winslet so I could feel her up while she was fighting for her life. We said, 'Deal!' they said, 'Action!' I got to feel up the comely Kate Winslet, and nobody ever heard of that poor bastard again. Name was

Vince Oberberger, I think. That's all I remember about Titanic's last victim."

"To what do you attribute your longevity?"

"Everything that didn't kill me only made me stronger. Either that or gave me one whopper of a hangover. But I persevered and I persevere still."

"At your advanced years, is there anything else you do remember?"

"Yes."

"Well?"

"The three things I've always remembered with absolute clarity are laughter, being born, and the day the music died."

"You remember being born? You're putting me on."

"It's true. I remember complete and perfect happiness one second and cold, naked — and I really mean naked — fear the next. Then I remember the doctor holding me by my feet and saying, 'It's a boy! A healthy baby boy!' I remember looking around the room and everyone was upside down and smiling at me. I remember being dumbfounded that I'd have to go through life upside down, but I smiled back because I didn't want to be labeled a troublemaking instigator. Then I remember this big son of a bitch taking his beefy hand and cracking me hard on the ass. I remember being hurt and mystified. I spent a good deal of my formative years believing being a healthy boy pleased them because they'd all get to watch the big doctor whack me on the ass. And this gratuitous violence was somehow pleasing to them. It wasn't until years later I learned that back then they whacked everybody on the ass. Healthy boy — whack! Healthy girl — whack! Unhealthy girl — whack! Unhealthy boy — whack! White, black — whack! Whack! It's safe to assume that unless you come out carrying a loaded revolver, chances are pretty good you're the one who's going to get whacked. The doctors back then said it was good for the baby, but I haven't trusted a single doctor since the precise second my butt started to sting. It was like the time I got stung on the ass by a hornet while I was racing naked through —"

"Stay on track, please. I don't have much time. You said you remember laughter."

"Yes, I do. I don't remember events, dates, presidents, lovers, the mundane or the magnificent, but I do remember laughter. All my life, it's as if someone's been tickling my ass with a giant invisible feather. Very pleasant. I assume God simply enjoys seeing my teeth and is intent on filling my life with laughter. I have no other explanation, but it's been wonderful, really."

"You don't have any teeth."

"Yes I do. That's them in the glass on the table. Now, if God wants to see my teeth He need only peek into the glass. I'm sure it's much simpler than tickling me with a giant invisible feather."

"Tell me about the day the music died."

"Ah, yes. It was 2039. I was getting all gassed up with the last surviving member of the Rolling Stones — say, you are familiar with the Stones aren't you?"

"I'm not here for a dialogue. Answer the question."

"Well, I'm not trying to be rude, but it's important because you can't have a party without the Stones. Anyway, the last surviving member of the Stones, the one who'd outlived all the others by two decades was ... gack? Gack? Gack! Gaacck! Gaaaaaaaaaaaa ..."

A violent seizure. Pandemonium ensued. The old golfer had taken one final stroke.

The nurses ran in. The docents ran out and the bratty and suddenly euphoric Girl Scout began fumbling for her camera phone. McCrae splashed face first into his Lucky Charms. The nurses checked his breathing. They checked his pulse. And because a camera was out, they all checked their makeup. A paramedic crew came crashing through the door.

One! Two! Three! They heaved him onto his back. The first paramedic took a needle attached to a small tube and put it in a tiny vein in the patient's left hand. The second took a needle with a slightly larger tube and put it in a pulsing blue vein in his right arm. A third paramedic took a tube about the circumference of a pencil and shoved it up a cavernous nostril. Then into the room came a slight, balding man toting what looked like an angry garden hose.

"All right, roll him over," he ordered.

McCrae, momentarily reviving at the threat of imminent penetration, hissed, "By God, you'd better not be thinking of sticking that thing up inside of me."

If you exclude the shouted expletive that followed insertion, these were widely reported to be his last words.

To Buster, those days seemed about a hundred years ago. Jarring lightning split the sky outside and he glanced at the monitors above McCrae's bed. The meaningless lines blipped and beeped with clinical indifference to the raging tempest. Paying customers were dripping puddles down the marbled hall and the more nervous types were jumping at each crack of the increasingly frequent bolts of blue lightning. On television, a game show contestant squealed in perfect synchronization with the lightning, almost as if it'd zapped her right on her nice, round bottom.

Then — CRACK!!! — she was gone. The building took a direct hit. Lights flickered and died. Alarmed, Buster glanced at the monitor above the prone man's bed. A look of pure joy crossed the face of the Louisville trucker who'd mistakenly allowed himself to believe it'd been McCrae, not the TV, that had tanked.

The lights on the monitor above the bed began to dim. McCrae, otherwise motionless for the past 18 months, gave a short start. His chest rose slowly and then settled back down again. An emergency generator kicked in seconds later. The blaring television filled the room with dysfunctional static. Buster ran to the hall, his heart pounding in his chest. "Dudash! Dudash! Get in here! Now!"

She was there in seconds, her face white as her uniform. "Is it over? Please, please, tell me this is finally over."

"No such luck. The lightning knocked out the satellite. Get up there and fix the television. That blonde's about to spin again."

Of course, Dudash knew less about television repair than she knew about critical nursing, which was less than nothing. She wasn't a nurse, the museum wasn't a hospital and McCrae wasn't a patient. There wasn't a single patient anywhere in the building. In fact, everyone was impatient and had been that way for more than five years. The people who waited in line were impatient. Dudash was impatient. Dingus was impatient. Staffers were impatient. The only soul in the entire Lucius B. Bolten Museum of Art and Natural History who seemed remotely patient was the serenely comatose McCrae. Enduring the endless crowds and the dirge-like monotony, McCrae seemed like a man with all the time in the world.

And that was the problem. He would not die. Alive and dying for the better part of five years, he just wouldn't get on with it.

The world had been hearing about baby boomers for nearly 150 years and the subject had grown tedious. A generation staring at itself in the mirror, baby boomers had always enjoyed the view. In the end, the world was so sick of them there was talk about hiring honest-to-goodness bounty hunters to track down the tired old remainders and shoot them off into deep space to fritter away their days angrily accusing one another of cheating at Euchre. But it was just rabble talk and one by one they all dried up and died off.

All except McCrae. And if you overlook the multitudes who were showing up year after year and around the clock to pray for his death, nobody wished him any ill. He was, after all, an intriguing subject. He'd enjoyed a life of spectacular failure exceeded only by dogged resilience. He'd never quit. He'd hit bottom more times than all but the most avid spankers, yet he always rose again.

And America took notice. He was as much a part of the nation's character as Uncle Sam himself. That's why they'd lodged him in a so-called "gallery suite" on the top floor of The Bolten Museum, a spectacular East 52rd Street tourist attraction named after the 53rd president of the United States, a former TV and movie star. People would come from all over the world to visit McCrae at his multimedia exhibit, one that was so interactive contestants would sometimes leave with inadvertent gobs of spit dripping from their faces, unwelcome residue from the subject's shouted declarations.

Prior to his coma, they could talk to him, ask him questions, have their picture taken with him, listen to his colorful lies and try to mine some truth from all the fool's gold spilling from his toothless mouth.

He'd lived an original life. He'd spent nearly two whole lifetimes warring against boredom and toward the end he'd simply surrendered to fatigue. That's when he met Buster Dingus. He'd been sitting on a park bench tending to the pigeons and thinking about all his dead friends. And that was everyone. Anyone and everyone he'd ever loved. They were all gone. All his friends, all his lovers, they'd all been vanquished by time. His dogs, the five Rexes, too, were all gone, including the beloved Nervous Rex and he missed him most of all.

Dead. All of them. He was alone. While all the others, everyone, had devoted themselves to living forever, by God, it looked like he was the only one who was going to have a real run at it. Living forever had been a national obsession. Eat right, don't drink, don't smoke, pop the right pills, and endure the self-torture that was daily exercise and you might escape death. So millions of healthy, strapping Americans led pristine, vice-free lives without blemish, profanity or flaw. In the end, that's what killed them. As the perfect specimens grew older and cruel time began to inflict its bitter victories against their brittle bodies, there was nothing the doctors could do to save them.

In the old days the doctor could tell patients to lose weight, quit smoking, stop drinking, control your anger, cut back on salt, drive carefully and pay the lady on their way out. But when the baby boomers got older all the doctors could say was, "I'm sorry. You've followed my best advice all your life and now there's nothing I can do for you. Pay the lady on your way out."

That's why doctors were thrilled with McCrae. His whole life he'd drank, smoked, ate rich foods, swore, had unsafe sex with lusty Haitians and generally lived a life of happy dissolution. While others were killing themselves trying to live forever, he'd done as he pleased. Now it was coming back to haunt him.

Five years earlier, he'd been reflecting upon this irony when he noticed the young man absentmindedly digging in his nose and staring at him. McCrae stuck a finger knuckle deep up his own booger barn and stared back, thus startling the young man into speech.

SEPTEMBER 2078

"You're McCrae, right?"

"Nope."

"Yes, you are. I recognize you. I saw you on TV. You're the last one. When you go, that's it. No more baby boomers."

"Please just scoot. I want to be left alone."

But the kid wouldn't scoot. He just kept staring at McCrae, who for months had been sitting at the same bench, feeding the same pigeons as he waited for tardy death to come by and pick him up the way passengers wait endlessly for the last, late bus home.

Buster had the face of a tombstone-toothed, badly carved pumpkin. His restless, amber eyes were rolling back and forth inside their sockets like tumbleweeds caught in a cross wind. His prematurely balding hair had a dark, Nixonian tuft slicked-down at the front, making it appear as if a skillful motorcyclist had burned rubber from his forehead clear back to the bald spot. He followed most remarks with nervous staccato laugh that sounded to Marty like someone had spilled a bucket of empty beer cans down a long flight of cement steps.

"I am an old man. I have little time left. In fact, I plan on dying here within the next few minutes. So, please, just go away."

"Look," Buster blurted out, "I think I know a way to make you a lot of money."

McCrae's surprised guffaw startled a few of the pigeons into an annoyed squawk.

"You think I need money? For what? My golden years? You are a foolish young man and I've had enough of fools. Now, go away. You're upsetting the pigeons."

Buster sensed opportunity, but the potter's wheel of his mind wasn't spinning fast enough to mold the clay into any thought that would hold water. He was the kind of guy who'd always preface deliberately insulting observations with, "I hope you won't take this as an insult ..." before delivering a devastating insult. Even as an adult, he looked like the kind of person who'd eat bugs for bucks. As a child, he was so lazy and utterly devoid of good intentions, his mother once paid him cash to stop stealing her jewelry. He still had his grandfather's bejeweled antique lighter, the sole survivor from the family haul he'd pawned long ago. Alien ambition had gnawed at him since he spied McCrae serenely feeding pigeons two days ago. A recently televised segment about McCrae had caught his interest for two reasons, and both of them were filling the swelled sweater of broadcaster Cherry Canyon. She was the stripper who'd scandalized the nation by sleeping with Vice President Timothy Wimple. He'd loved her madly until she was stricken by what the wags called the "Boobonic Plague." The inexplicable medical condition had mysteriously rendered women with voluptuously enhanced breasts with equivalently enhanced intelligence, thus making them wholly unsuitable playthings to superficial men who'd long pawed after the sort. Then, for Wimple at least, everything went straight to hell. He became the butt of jokes, President Cochran gave him nothing to do, and his wife and family were cold and distant. In short, absolutely nothing had changed except the carrot-topped Cherry came to despise him as a simple dolt and wanted nothing more to do with him, and he sorely missed her cuddles.

For Cherry and thousands of other women, the Boobonic Plague was a godsend. She wrote a thoughtful book about the affair, was hailed for her wit and insight. Deep pocket producers gave her a television show of her own. Women liked her because she was sassy, forthright and disrespectful to males. Men admired her more visible qualities but generally preferred to watch her program with the sound turned down because of her tendency to say hurtful truths about their gender.

It was Cherry Canyon who, besides her ample cleavage, revealed on national television that McCrae was still alive and was indeed the last living baby boomer. She produced his birth certificate — born Dec. 9, 1964, Passavant Hospital, Pittsburgh — he was 113 years old; she checked with the rosy-cheeked and cheerful Maxwell Barnacle, a government census official who, after some overly-dramatic calculations said, indeed, McCrae was the last living baby boomer. The final 15 minutes of the show featured footage of McCrae angrily refusing to be interviewed, slamming doors on Barney, Cherry's refrigerator-sized sidekick cameraman, whacking Barney with the silver handle of his walnut cane, flipping the bird at Barney, mooning Barney, shooting bullets wildly in Barney's direction, siccing his rabid monkey on Barney, and pouring boiling oil on Barney from the roof of his small brownstone.

The show drew huge ratings because all the promos showed the indestructible Barney taking a terrific beating and because it was Cherry-Wears-A-Halter-Top Wednesday and viewers always tuned in to see Cherry in a halter top. It was always considered a grabber, particularly this night when the show concluded with McCrae being a grabber in the final scene where he made a lustful lunge at Cherry's canyon before sprawling helplessly on the sidewalk while she signed off from above the supine senior with, "And be sure to tune in Friday when I'll do the news dressed like a French maid!"

The immediate result of the report was for office and Internet ghoul pools to be flooded with the name Martin J. McCrae, greatly depressing the odds of anyone hitting for much. Everywhere people bubbled with enthusiasm that the boomers might finally die off and with amazement that McCrae was still spry enough to make a sporting leap at Cherry's silicone valley.

That Buster was thinking nothing of halters, cleavage, French maids or humiliated cameramen was a tribute to the power of the idea that had germinated in him the day of the report and was now bursting like a beanstalk through the fertile manure of his mind. He understood that for the better part of the past century, everyone who breathed was either a Baby Boomer or despised scores of them. It was a can't miss sort of demographic. To him, McCrae was the ultimate ghoul pool, the culmination of a generation's endless obsession with youth and the grim resistance to its final fate.

But his sole moment of genius would wither without the cooperation of the decrepit old Crankenstein. His shot depended on securing the willing participation of a cantankerous old man who not only had no reason to live and could, in fact, make a compelling argument in favor of a quick suicidal demise.

"All right, you don't need money," he said. "But you could leave it to someone, a relative, a charity. You could do someone a lot of good."

"There is no one. I am alone, utterly vanquished. My relations have all deserted me. I'm mistrustful of charities. There is no one I care to enrich and my dear monkey fled after it was maced by Barney." He was thoughtfully silent for a moment. "All I have are these pigeons. They are good company and I wish them well. But they don't need money. They don't even need me. When I'm gone, someone else will feed them. And if no one feeds them, they'll still survive. They're perfectly independent. Tell me, have you ever seen a skinny pigeon? An old pigeon? A baby pigeon? A pigeon nest? A pigeon egg? A sick pigeon? A dead one? A pigeon that didn't look almost exactly like every other damned pigeon? No. For all we know they live forever. The world might have an assigned number of pigeons that have been here since Noah. Kings, dynasties, nations — they come and they go. But the pigeons remain. The very same pigeons. These pigeons might have been in the rafters at old Yankee Stadium when the great DiMaggio danced across center field. These might be the same pigeons who were there when the pilgrims and the Indians enjoyed the first Thanksgiving.

They may have been there when the Romans nailed Christ to the cross. No one ever thinks about that. The poets never write about the pigeons. The artists never paint them. But they were there. I guarantee it."

He looked as if he were about to shed a sentimental tear on behalf of the pigeons. He turned thoughtful and said to Buster, "If you have money, would you please consider making a machine that would decipher what a pigeon has to say? It might fascinate."

Buster stood slack-jawed in wonder. "You're right. I have never devoted a second of thought to a pigeon. But I'll tell you this, any man who's devoted that much time to thinking about pigeons may not need money, but he needs someone to talk to besides these damn gutter birds. You're bored. I know about you. I know about your life. What you've done, who you knew. You shouldn't be sitting here spending your last days analyzing the posterity of pigeons."

McCrae gently cocked his head. The fall breezes blew the shoulder-length white hair in wispy swirls around his lightly bearded face. Time, gravity and a dainty diet of Cajun rice and beans had dwindled his once robust 5-foot-9, 185-pound frame to a stooped, fragile, 5-foot-6, 108-pounds. His face was as wrinkled and craggy as a topographical map of the Rockies. If every line told a story, then his face was prolific as the Library of Congress. He asked, "And what should I be doing?"

"You should be making history."

McCrae snorted. "Did my share of that. You must have slept through class that day."

Here was a man who couldn't be bought, bribed, coerced, cajoled or blackmailed into doing something he did not wish to do. McCrae, perhaps for the first time in his life, was beyond corrupting. Buster felt like strangling him for it.

What do you give the man who has everything but time?

All it takes in life to be successful, even massively so, is just one good idea. Buster had his in front of McCrae and his pigeons. "Mr. McCrae, you're bored out of your mind. You've golfed with five presidents, danced with princesses and you've raced balloons across the Sea of Tranquility. You've surfed rivers of lava, ran with the bulls and rode the first elevator to the top of Everest. And now you're bored to death. Well, I have the cure for all your boredom."

"What do you have in mind?"

Buster looked him square in the eye and said, "I'd like to take you and put you in a museum and charge people to come see you. And since you're the last baby boomer on Earth and the oldest man on the planet, I'd like to run a lottery ghoul pool so that whoever is in the room with you when you finally die wins all the loot."

It came out in such a torrent, Buster didn't have time to dam any of it up with even a veil of subtle tact. It just spilled out and drenched McCrae. If the pigeons were surprised by the proposal, they didn't let on.

⚜

It was outrageous. It was unsavory. It was the kind of thing that made decent people everywhere cringe in disgust. McCrae embraced it almost immediately. After a long moment of silent reflection where Buster thought the subject of his sole moment of inspiration had passed to his final reward, McCrae's eyes sprang open and he climbed on board with a chipper, "Oh, what the hell. I'll do it! Now, let's go grab a beer! It's on you."

The ghoul pool had always been central to his life and philosophy. Who was next to die? While others shunned death and the morbid mention of it, McCrae had always embraced it. Anytime he heard of anyone dying suddenly, it gave him an urgent drive to ensure he'd live more suddenly.

He'd always enjoyed ghoul pools and had an uncanny eye for impassively picking who'd be the next to slip into the great unknown. He'd accurately predicted the deaths of famous musicians, politicians, artists, local scoundrels, beloved bar owners, fast-living young actors, celebrated clergy and in 2016 a prized thoroughbred that snapped a foreleg down the homestretch at Churchill Downs.

Of course, throughout his life, the name Martin J. McCrae had always been at the top of many ghoul pools because he recklessly engaged in many of the high-risk activities that claimed the lives of so many others.

"I don't want to live forever," he say. "I want to live right now!" That's what he'd always say when asked why he lived like he did. Now he'd put himself in the ultimate ghoul pool. He'd leapt into an irresistible American vortex of greed, crass consumerism, shrill spectacle and fickle chance and ensured he'd be the one to lead the entire planet screaming behind him clear to the very pit of it all.

During the weeks that followed, he instructed Dingus to make all the arrangements. He insisted on being kept informed of all the details concerning his comfort, care and what size television would be in the room. He would be an exhibit. A piece. People could come and watch him and talk to him if he felt like talking back. The Hygiene Comfort

Clean 2500 adjustable bed would address all personal needs with dainty dispatch. The state-of-the-art machine a veritable potty palace that could wipe, dry, dispose and sanitize of all McCrae's wastes with the nimble dispatch of a squad of British nannies. A small commode was behind Buster's plush chair, but Buster was the only one who used it and he was in it so infrequently he rarely had time to do anything but look at the pictures in all the porno magazines he kept stuffed under a cabinet in there the way he used to keep the same skin diversions back when he was a kid.

If McCrae chose to, he'd never have to get up out of bed again.

Sponsors were quick to climb on board. Historians were already writing the final mark of the baby boomers would be tastelessness, hysteria and gaudy excess. To their grandchildren, nothing was so funny as watching baby boomers age. Just the names produced snorts of oxymoronic giggles. Septuagenarian Baby Boomer. Patrician Baby Boomer. The sociologists meant no harm when they dubbed the horde of runny-nosed postwar spawn "baby boomers," but you can't attach the name "baby" to an entire generation and not expect some psychological warping. It's like calling the little neighbor kid Stinky and not expecting him to grow up distant and awkward around the ladies.

So as the decades passed and these cherubic babies began to become sagging adults with knees that clicked, breasts that drooped, hairlines that rose and peckers that didn't, they went to comical lengths to fend off aging or at least the appearance of it. They nearly bankrupted the country by pulling all their money out of their 401-K plans and throwing it at squads of eager young plastic surgeons promising miracle cures for crow's feet, unsightly age spots and the brewer's droop. The immediate effect of these transactions was to plunge destitute Wall Street into recession, make tycoons out of cosmetic surgeons and a sad shambles of the mortician industry.

Who needs funeral directors when the dead have been embalmed five years prior to burial?

Condensing the whole generation into one Caligulian festival of excess — soon dubbed *"EXCESSTIVAL!!!"* — seemed entirely appropriate. A host of dignitaries read prepared speeches as the cameras focused on McCrae, who appeared frightened and near death, a fact that was conveyed with gaudy detail on the eight-story JumboTron towering over Times Square. The wanton revelry had terrified the ancient McCrae. Had Buster refused his pleas for a tranquilizer and a pint of bourbon, it's doubtful he'd have been able to even make it to the stage.

With eyes like galaxies, the image of McCrae stared out at the crowd that stared straight back at him. His was a face that fascinated and here it was, finally, as big as the city itself. People marveled at the sweeping canyons around his mouth, the rivers of dimples that plunged across his cheek and the crow's feet so deep and expressive, they appeared to be capable of taking flight. Once raging scars on his forehead looked like mountain ranges and the throbbing mole on his left cheek looked like it could comfortably accommodate the drunken crowd attending a professional hockey game. It was a face that belonged in a museum for no other reason than it was, perhaps, the last adult face on the face of the Earth that hadn't undergone a single procedure at the hands of even a clumsy multi-thumbed, hillbilly plastic surgeon.

He felt a gush of gratitude when the nightmare ended and Buster agreed to let him take a robust blast of booze while leading him to the convertible that would whisk him to where he was destined to spend his final days on Earth. The posh new Lucius B. Bolten Museum had been selected because the Bolten was a lasting monument to the excesses of the Baby Boom generation that had elected a beloved sitcom actor president. Bolten, who'd never even bothered to run for office, was elected while doing a sitcom in which he portrayed a candidate running for office.

This was a fitting career trajectory for an actor that voting viewers remember as having been a conservative young man growing up in a wacky family. The role showed him as an informed youth unafraid of tackling tough issues. This scored well with voters. Then, logically, he played a political consultant with a wacky cast of office mates with whom he helped run New York. From this, voters inferred he had hands-on practical experience with the nitty-gritty of local government that would keep the streets safe and clean. As he matured into adulthood, the still youthful-looking actor played, in succession: an ambassador to a wacky banana boat republic; a junior senator from a leading dairy-producing state with a cast of wacky talking farm animals; and finally, as himself, he played a presidential candidate grappling with the tough issues in a campaign dominated by wacky voters.

The show was so successful and the candidate, at least in the minds of viewers, so qualified that no one was surprised when Bolten's name showed up on ballots nationwide and the popular actor was soon ushered into the White House in the landslide of 2032. Everyone was satisfied with the outcome, until the premise for the show shifted from the campaign trail to the White House. Poll numbers dipped until Bolten, who saw no reason to step down as the show's executive producer, appointed a wacky talking cow as Secretary of Defense and had it declare war on a wacky banana boat republic, which was a huge ratings success and led to Bolten's reelection in 2036.

So it made perfect sense to lodge McCrae in the Bolten penthouse gallery at the namesake museum that had become the nation's attic for all things Baby Boomer. When the baby boomers began to die, their descendants willed their vast collections of Brady Bunch lunch boxes, Star Wars action figures and vinyl LP folk art to the Bolten Foundation.

McCrae willed himself.

"I like the view," he said as he tottered into the spartan room where he would be spending his final moments on Earth. Unlike the gaudy displays scattered throughout the Bolten, McCrae's suite was white as a stack of fresh tombstones. The walls were bare of artistic enhancement; nothing in the room proper would distract from the center of attention with the personality still dazzling enough to seem psychedelic.

He'd made a few suggestions, but had been a model patient/guest/exhibit whatever — no one could agree on what to call him. Buster would do his bidding. Excesstival had given the country a happy lift and had made Buster a prominent man, sought for interviews and influence. And it would make someone else fabulously wealthy. It had the potential to become the biggest jackpot in history.

Some said it would get as high as $300 million. Although some deemed the $14 admission, plus the $25 ticket to take a chance on McCrae, as too cost prohibitive, Buster had the museum construct the 440-foot Death Chute so that, in addition to the lottery ticket, losers would still get to enjoy a Disney-worthy thrill ride that deposited them on the sidewalk right next to the gift shop's bargain rack. The jackpot would be further bloated by off-site gamblers who were wagering millions on the widespread conviction that he could go at any minute. Clever bookmakers in Las Vegas were also assisting Buster in arranging wagers that let bettors gamble on the exact day he'd die. Crazy and unexpected prop bets — offbeat propositions that any number of embarrassing or unexpected instances would happen — became commentary fodder that raged across the social media. Bets included whether more women than men would play; which celebrities would visit the most often or not at all; and whether any legally-permitted guide dogs would spray urine on McCrae or vice versa.

And with every wager, Buster was getting a cut.

He'd been whispering to friends that McCrae would not last three weeks. Not that he was telling any secrets. Doctors said they were surprised to see McCrae even upright, let alone planning for the future. Of the doctors who were assigned to monitor him, two said his heart would fail, three predicted stroke and one said convincingly on the noon news, "Old age will kill him. It's not just that the man's 113, he's an old 113. It's like a car with a lot of miles on it. You take it to the shop and they tell you they could fix the carburetor, but then they'd have to replace the fuel injectors, and if they do that they'll have to strip the engine, and on and on and on. There's just nothing they can do. That's McCrae, except with a car you can at least disassemble it and use it for parts. Not this guy. His parts are worthless, even to him, for the most part. Frankly, I wouldn't transplant his diseased liver into a sick pig. It'd be too cruel to the poor pig."

There was a slight tapping on the door. Dingus and McCrae turned from the window to see Bolten Museum special event curator Holly Vanwig standing with a statuesque brunette in blue jeans and a pulse-quickening sweater. "Mr. Dingus, Mr. McCrae, this is Becky Dudash. We've hired her to be your nurse."

"Nice to meetcha," Buster said with a perfunctory nod. He had much on his mind. In one week, more than 20.5 million one dollar tickets had been sold on Earth and the seven inhabited planets and moons in the known universe. Only on Gonto, the idyllic Alpha Centauri moon that McCrae had saved from civilization, had not a single ticket been purchased. The undiscovered colony of mono-armed tree-dwellers revered McCrae and would forever cherish his memory.

McCrae'd loved his two years on Gonto as much as he'd loved anything in his entire life. His only regret about his years there was that he'd just missed Jesus by two days. Two days! God, he would have loved to have met Jesus.

McCrae's death, if he lived the four hours it would take for the contest to officially begin, would enrich two winners. The person holding a ticket corresponding to the randomly drawn number at the time of death would take $20 million. The big money and the king's ransom of prizes would go to the person standing in the room when McCrae was declared dead. The historic first player was Emily Pennington, a demure sugar cookie of 12-year-old innocence from Eugene, Oregon. Photographers would snap her picture as the smiling sixth-grader became the first contestant through the door to spend 14 minutes and 59.5 seconds with the — Dingus hoped — chatty McCrae. Sweet Emmy Pennington was at that very moment saying earnest prayers that McCrae would drop stone dead in precisely three hours and 49 minutes, give or take a charitable minute or two.

While the details of this were ricocheting maddeningly around Dingus's brain, McCrae was slowly entering the third stage of his intoxication, that of a charmingly adolescent 112-year-old. Bending to kiss her ivory hand, he said, "How do you do, Ms. Dudash? It is indeed a pleasure to meet you."

Dudash, charmed by the courtliness of the gesture, felt an immediate rush of sweet affection for the old man whose wrinkled and weather-beaten skin resembled to less refined observers the gnarled bark on the giant sequoias. Of 127 female and 42 male applicants, Dudash was deemed perfect for the role of nurse, a position which required not a single nursing skill. She was told right up front it would be a short-term role and she'd likely be out of work within two to four months. The timing of her arrival was a happy coincidence for McCrae, who was within another snort or two from entering the crying-about-your-daddy phase of his drunkenness, a stage from which it is virtually impossible to make a favorable impression on anyone except your long-dead daddy.

"It's nice to meet you, Mr. McCrae."

"Please, call me Marty. Everyone else does. Just Marty."

"Marty it is. I'm looking forward to spending a lot of time with you, and hearing your stories. You've led an amazing life."

Marty smiled serenely.

Vanwig said, "Becky'll be on duty all day at the desk across the hall. She'll be dressed like a nurse, but mainly, she'll do housekeeping, order your food and see to your comfort. She'll be here full-time. When she's not here, museum staffers will see to your needs."

"Dudash, I must say, you sort of favor Isabella, my fourth wife. Is there any connection between the Dudash line and the Louisiana Boudreaus?"

"No, not that I know of."

"Now, Marty," Vanwig broke in, "all our research indicates your fourth and seventh wives were black women. Becky, as you can surely see is a fair-skinned Caucasian. The two don't look at all alike. Don't think of playing any little games with this young girl's head. We can't have you chasing off the help with your devilish ways."

"Ah, Mrs. Vanwig, you are correct, as usual. Isabella was indeed black as a pilgrim's church britches. I remember it now. Boy, what a lusty, passionate woman she was, that one. I'll never forget the night we met. Five times we made love under the bayou moon. I remember waking up the next day with mosquito bites on my ass and a dented wedding ring on my finger. I could explain the bites, but I doubt Sherlock Holmes could have explained the arrival of the ring. In fact, some of those bites outlasted the marriage."

Vanwig shook her head in a slow scold. "Becky, you'll have your hands full with Marty. He says and does as he pleases. I'll leave it to you to watch your step."

Dudash didn't mind. "Oh, I think we'll get along fine," she said, unconsciously picking up a pillow from the couch and fluffing it with a couple of quick, smart jabs. "I want to hear all his stories about the people he knew, the places he's been and things he's done. You're one of the most fascinating people from the last 200 years. And here you are, even after 112 years, still making history. Amazing."

He ambled over to the window and looked out at the horizon. The wrinkled corners of his mouth smiled sunshine and he turned to Dudash and said, "Darlin', you ain't seen nothin' yet. Right Buster?"

"Right on, boss man."

McCrae's right arm had drifted to the pocket under his coat. Vanwig sprung too late to prevent the old man from tilting the concealed bottle into his smiling maw, quickly draining the amber contents clear down to the drippings.

"Martin Jacob McCrae! You give me that bottle. Oh, you are a rascal!"

Dabbing the corners of his mouth with his sleeve, McCrae gave a satisfied shudder and with a fragrant belch motioned to Dudash. "Come, let's sit together on the couch. I want to tell you about my daddy."

⟶⧼⧽⟿

In those early days, back when anyone still cared about such humanitarian niceties, contestants were X-rayed, photographed, eye scanned, fingerprinted, issued ID cards, drug tested and radiated to kill any infectious organisms, bugs or slugs that might be used to slay McCrae. Each person was made to pass through both metal and mental detectors because, although everyone wanted him dead, nobody wanted him killed. That would be unfair so elaborate precautions were made to secure a safe, natural death.

He would receive only the most meager of medical assistance. Nurse Dudash was there merely for cosmetic purposes. Early on, a paramedic crew was on call, too, but that all ended after the coma when everybody was just hoping McCrae would die and they could all just get on with it.

A certified board panel of medical ethicists oversaw his care. They determined that if McCrae complained of pain, his suffering would be minimized. But if his heart stopped, there would be no resuscitation. The only invasive procedures that would ever trouble the mortal McCrae again would be the unhindered irrigation of nasal, anal, and urinary ports, most of which would be undertaken, again, for purely cosmetic reasons. About the generally uncontrolled flatulence, they would do nothing but hold their breath around McCrae. Despite ventilation and perfumed aroma assisters, McCrae's loud, noxious farts would produce snorts of giggles and despair throughout the duration of the contest.

"Well, doctors, I think that takes care of everything," said Dr. Percival Priest, at the final meeting of the esteemed ethics board. "Does anyone have anything else?"

In the back row Dr. Jack Chester cleared his throat and slowly rose to address his colleagues. "Has anyone given any thought to the ethics of gambling on the death of a sick old man simply for the base gratification of sport and profit? I mean shouldn't we at least discuss the morality of this whole Excesstival and, perhaps, take a reasoned stand on it? Really, ladies and gentlemen, consider: Is this what we've become, a sanction to this morose pathetic death watch of a once vital human being?"

Some of the finest, most learned doctors and ethicists in the medical profession turned as one and poured their puzzled stares on Chester. He held their rapt gaze for a full 10 seconds before his face finally broke.

The room erupted in laughter.

"You dang joker!" Priest said. "You really had me going there! All right, all right. Meeting adjourned, bar's open. Now, somebody bring me a Scotch, neat!"

With those moral refinements safely tucked aside, the great beast roared to life and on October 5, 2076, it was game on. Into the maw marched the ceaseless multitudes. They came in by themselves, in pairs, in chaperoned groups and in massive hovercraft minivans fueled with hydrogen batteries the size of antique hearing aids. They came in masses huddled, tired, rich and poor. They came seeking endorsements, enlightenment and universally they came seeking instant riches. A jackpot that would commence at $21.5 million and would swell exponentially hour by hour and serve to lure both the needy and the greedy.

Their spent avarice kindled McCrae's competitive fires. Always stubborn, his constitution became fortified with every prayer he die. Most people live their lives in bitter pursuit of elusive riches. McCrae finally had what he'd most wanted his whole life.

He finally had an audience. He finally had an opportunity to fulfill the need that had for his entire life consumed his every waking moment. He would be heard. He would expound on any matter that popped into his brain. If he wanted to wonder if the Marines had to march through Singoli and Douboli before they got to Tripoli, he'd do it. If he wanted to explain why one of his life's greatest disappointments was learning the titmouse was neither tit nor mouse, the topic would dominate the conversation. He could affix brain barnacles on a thousand consecutive strangers by telling them that, while pending armageddon would be cataclysmic, anatomically speaking it would get its butt kicked by legmageddon. He was certain with enough persistence and ears he could sway the entire mass culture into referring to former brothels that had evolved into trendy lodging spots as "ho'tels." He could now could tell anyone who approached, truth be damned that he swore he'd recently met a man on a chilly morning who was wearing a musical bellows across his chest and that, by God, that man was dressed accordioningly.

"If fans of the Grateful Dead," McCrae would wonder, "are called Deadheads, then what does that make those of us who revere Moby Dick?"

He asked a fashionable young actress with an obvious shoe fetish how man, the only animal that spends 65 percent of its entire existence seated on its ass is also the only one that spends billions of dollars each year on fancy footwear.

He had an opportunity to set a national conversation that he'd believed had rambled on far too incoherently for his liking.

As for the prayers, the customers might as well have been praying to deified bars of soap. It was as if God had taken the weekend off, put His feet up and was going to sit back and enjoy the show. Thus, it became one of the few times during his long mortal duration that McCrae and the

Almighty were truly on the same page, sharing the same rooting interests. Despite the prayers, the show was destined to go on and on and on.

It was during the third day of the third week that Paul Armey, great-grandson of his old friend Skip Armey paid his $25, placed his side bets and introduced himself to McCrae. Marty'd been friends with the late Skip since they were freshman at Ohio University. He'd been a top pitching prospect who'd lost his left arm in a train accident when he, Marty and Buddy Allman had played hobo one drunken weekend and Skip fell under the wheels of the an Akron-bound CSX freighter. The northbound train severed the southpaw's golden limb just south of the shoulder. His pitching days were over. He'd died in 2052, Marty remembered. Marty'd gone to visit him in the nursing home where diabetes had robbed him of both legs just below the knees. Marty noted that the boy who'd been born with four limbs and named Skip would die with just one and be confined to a wheelchair. The nurses were uniformly horrified at Marty's suggestion that everyone should start calling Skip by the name Rollie. Even legless, Skip still got what he said was a "kick" out of it.

Paul Armey said his mother had told him that Skip had been one of the meanest, most profane and spiteful men she'd ever met. "She said he couldn't be trusted," Paul remarked, shaking his head. "She said the only time she ever saw him happy was when he saw others in pain or conflict. Just a nasty, nasty man, is what she said."

Marty wholeheartedly agreed and felt a warm wistfulness at the recollection of a man he'd beloved for many of those same reasons. Marty knew of no one who'd understood the essence of life better than Skip, who when Marty asked him to come up with the most negative statement about the meaning of life said, "A series of disappointments, each one greater than the last, leading inexorably to the grave."

Marty thought that was hilarious.

He'd forget the faces and names of the myriad countless contestants who'd come to gamble and go away, but he never forgot the confused look on Paul Armey's face when Marty recalled about how much fun it was to be around someone who could be counted upon to corrupt any human innocence with sarcasm and ridicule. He didn't know whether the reverie the young Armey triggered with his recollections were the reason or not, but that night was when the dreams that carried him through clear to the very end first began.

IN DREAMVILLE ...

The recurring dreams always began the instant he entered slobber sleep. He hadn't been a slobber sleeper in more than 30 years and wondered if the return of soulful, sloppy, slobber sleep meant the end was nigh. He hoped it did. True slobber sleep to him was heaven.

He didn't know if he dreamed of the donkey in the sombrero because it was there or because he always just wanted to dream about donkeys in sombreros. He didn't know whether dream interpretation made any sense or was just crap, but he thought a shrink, fortune teller or bar stool Socrates could have a lot of fun trying to explain the meaning of a donkey in a sombrero. He'd always enjoyed Mexican food, siestas, margaritas and mariachi music in cantinas by the beach. He thought those were things a companionable donkey wearing a sombrero would enjoy, too.

The donkey didn't do or say anything. It just stood there on the side of the stage in the big auditorium. It would on occasion bend to nibble from a pile of some hay that had been strewn at her hooves. The auditorium was filled with about 200 eager faces in neat rows that reminded him of the sociology classes in which he'd slobber slept through as a freshman back in Athens, Ohio. A vacant podium and microphone was stage left. He was seated stage right in a comfortable chair.

He knew people who had chased love and money all their lives and had died unhappy. Once he'd hit 50, all he'd ever sought from life was a really comfortable chair. And in his dream, he'd found a doozy. It was royal blue. It had plush piled velour upholstery and a high back with lower lumbar cushioned support. The arm rests had the firm, supple feel of bags full of stale marshmallows. Sitting in it, he'd felt in his dreams like he'd collapsed into a giant blue breast.

A really good comfortable chair has a lazy inertia all its own. For it to really work, people needed to at first resist it the way they did forbidden opiates. Like forbidden opiates, people needed to be wary of a good chair because committing to it could wipe out an afternoon's worth of labored productivity.

And that was perfectly fine with Marty.

The yin and yang of a chair's Lazy Boy inertia was that once you succumbed to it, it had a way of enveloping you and banishing all your busiest motivations, much the way, say, a giant blue breast would to men like Marty

And the same could be said, he felt, about a good glass of bourbon and a long cigar. When he began pairing the two in about 2001, Marty knew he'd found friends for life. He was a new father at the time and was struck by how sipping good bourbon and smoking a fine cigar hit the exact same spot in his brain as it did holding a new baby. He didn't know if that made him a bad father or a really good drinker. He just knew the sensations were the same. He'd eventually stop holding babies, but he never set down a good cigar and a glass of bourbon on ice. They were fine companions, the Batman and Robin of ambition-bashing splendors.

In his dream he looked to his side and, lo and behold, there was a bottle of Jack Daniel's Tennessee sippin' whiskey, an ice bucket, a box of Cohiba Churchills, a cutter and a fancy propane lighter that looked powerful enough to defoliate a forest. At arm height and to his right side, his smoking side, was an antique ash tray. A cigar to him was an hour-long commitment to absolute idleness, his default social posture.

"This," he thought, "is gonna be sublime."

As the audience continued its chipper chatter, Marty reached over and liberated three heavy ice cubes from the bucket and dropped them into the glass. He opened the bottle and let the bourbon splash over the ice. It made satisfied crackles as the warm amber whiskey tumbled onto the ice and caused it to fracture. He filled it clear up. Then he reached over and snipped the end off a Cohiba so fresh it felt like moist mulch straight from the garden. He lit up and took a deep draw. He'd resolved in 2012 that before the year was out he'd master the art of blowing smoke rings. And he did. He blew three smoke rings so perfectly circular he sensed observers in the audience could have envisioned a chorus line of Rockettes hula hooping through the trio of smokey ghosts.

He was just beginning to wonder if he should address the audience when the lights dimmed and the crowd hushed. The stage was basked in warm theatrical lighting. Then, just past the donkey in the sombrero, he saw Buddy emerge.

Buddy Allman was the best friend he'd ever had in a life that was crowded with splendid friendships the way toll plazas are crowded with traffic during rush hours. He rarely spoke and when he did what he said was imbued with uncommon wisdom. They'd become friends after he'd overheard Buddy telling a young art major he dreamed of opening an art gallery with bare walls and 40 guys inside who'd do nothing but introduce themselves to patrons by saying, "Hi, I'm Art."

Brilliant, Marty thought. They'd be friends forever.

He was dressed in a dapper purple smoking jacket with that dazzled in the spotlight. Death, at least in dreams, had been good to him. He looked fit and robust and Marty hadn't seen him look like that from about the day they'd met. It was the Buddy he remembered from before the instant he became the Buddy he'd never knew.

He'd had more laughs with Buddy than any other human being on the planet. He was the warmest, most fun man he'd ever known. They were like brothers. Buddy's pointless suicide in 2032 was the saddest day of his life and caused a grief tsunami that had never ebbed. So he was thrilled to see Buddy, alive and well, even if it was only in Dreamville.

Buddy, bourbon and cigars! Throw in a little slobber sleep when the booze and butts were all spent and maybe he was in heaven.

Buddy patted the donkey, gave it a carrot, smiled at Marty and took up a position behind the podium at center stage. Then he turned and nodded to an usher wearing a red coat and standing in the aisle in front of Marty.

Through the smoke, Marty could see all the people he'd ever loved and disappointed. They were lined up and getting ready to one by one take their turns on the stage.

And they all looked like they had something to say.

NOVEMBER 2078

A key to the early success of what everyone agreed was the most ghoulish ghoul pool in history, the world's most stupendous and ballyhooed reality show, was McCrae's surreal vivacity. He slept fewer than three hours a night, was wittily conversational throughout the day, and often surprised contestants by springing out of bed to shake their hands, pose for pictures and titillate each and every one of the females by giving them a playful goose cunningly timed to coincide with the instant the pictures were snapped.

Nothing phased him. When evaluators told him he'd need to undergo a long and painful colonoscopy, his wry response made headlines around the world: "McCrae on Colonoscopy: 'Bummer!'"

His behavior was a tonic in a world that for so long dreaded growing old that minds had calcified into thinking The Golden Years were nothing but rusted dread. Even those who'd had no interest in the ghoul pool, were lining up en masse simply to see this frisky specimen seizing each moment of every day with zesty gusto. That one old man could be so extravagantly imbued with exuberance left even misshapen pessimists strolling away feeling a vicarious jolt.

Medical experts who'd assured reporters that he'd be dead within a month or two began to issue backpedaling revisions stating that the surge of vitality was likely due to the daily adrenal rush of being part of something so historic and dazzling that death had become an afterthought.

Buster saw it everyday. People wanted to hug him in the hopes that some of the magic would stick to them. And McCrae was more than glad to reciprocate. He hugged, he squeezed, he embraced. And he talked.

And talked.

Buster, whose raspy voice sounded like he'd gargled with sandpaper cereal, was amazed at the volume, clarity and expansiveness of McCrae's chats.

His whole life Marty'd been capable of talking all the ears off acres of corn. But that ability was often dashed when many of the ears he was talking to, would get off their bar stools and simply stroll away. Here in the Bolten Museum, he was in a room he'd never again leave, but he had a captive audience, one person at a time. Everybody had a question and he was never at a loss for answers.

"I've read that you never concerned yourself with money," said a 35-year-old bullet train conductor from Kansas in New York for the afternoon run. "Is that true?"

"Not at all," McCrae said. "I used to gloomily pursue wealth to the point where I'd wake up in the middle of the night wondering why I wasn't prosperous. I'd pray about it."

"Were your prayers ever answered?"

"In a way," McCrae said, "and this was the key: I used to pray for riches and get nothing. Then I began praying for wisdom and needed nothing."

A middle-aged divorcee who ran a combination hair salon/bait shop in New Mexico said she was struggling with raising a son and that her own checkered past made finding the right words difficult. McCrae smiled and serenely intoned: "Simply tell him that those who do right can never go wrong."

When a 47-year-old from Cleveland said he was considering going from banking to baking, a peace-of-mind job shift that might imperil his family's lifestyle, McCrae counseled, "We are born free and spend the rest of our lives constructing prisons around ourselves. Perhaps you've earned yourself a life-stress parole."

To Buster, it seemed he had a facile ability to turn himself into a walking fortune cookie. He said porn directors were the only people who should ever be allowed to shout, "Man up!" He'd warn pre-med students if they did nothing but study anatomy they were bound to wind up real know bodies. He'd tell dedicated entomologists they couldn't help but be anything other than bug-eyed and he'd insist it was entirely possible for someone who ate nothing but doughnuts, cheeseburgers and pepperoni pizza throughout the day to boast they'd had a well-rounded diet.

Often these thought provokers made their way into the local news outlets. In fact, blogs dedicated to McCrae's wisdoms began popping up with such regularity that Buster had lawyers begin copywriting McCrae's pronouncements for retail reasons. That meant everyone using material gleaned from meeting with McCrae would have to pay Buster a 10 percent cut.

Everyone but Penelope Hart.

McCrae had fallen in love with her over a week's time when she'd come in on a daily basis to study him and the effects on media attention on aging for a doctoral thesis she was preparing for her pre-med studies at Columbia University.

Her eyes, McCrae thought, were as dark and inviting as brim-filled cups of steaming cappuccino. The memory of her sunshine smile beneath a tumultuous tumble of light brown curls would have sustained an astronaut through six months of deep space isolation. McCrae saw her and impulsively proposed that she become his 14th and final wife. She was 23. His status as a sporting optimist was enhanced when he told reporters that he didn't think the circumstances and their 90-year-age discrepancy would make much of a difference.

Plus, he'd forever harbored an ambition to date a girl named Penelope. He'd spent his entire life stooping to pick up the world's most inconsequential coin, often earning glares of scorn from busier pedestrians, and now he had an opportunity to pick up a Penny that was really worth something.

He loved her because her first question went right to the heart of what he'd been trying to do his entire life.

"So, tell me," she said, "how does one live such a colorful life?"

He looked straight into her dark eyes and without hesitation replied, "You use all the crayons."

And with that he was off. He began by recalling, without notes or prompts, that when Joseph Binney founded Peekskill Chemical Works in 1864, the company that would grow to be Crayola Crayons produced just two colors: Charcoal and Lamp Black, "and it took a discerning eye to differentiate between the two. Children today can choose from hundreds of different colors like Laser Lemon or Tickle Me Pink. We can paint our lives as brightly or dimly as we choose. But through life, some of us lose or wear down some of our more dazzling colors, living each and every day as if it were either Charcoal or Lamp Black. I never lived a day as if were either Charcoal or Lamp Black when I could spackle it with some Mauvelous Mauve or some Atomic Tangerine."

She stood with her hands on hips and said, "I'm perfectly charmed by your analogy."

His chestnut brown eyes gave her their most captivating laser gaze and he said, "And I am perfectly charmed that you're perfectly charmed."

"Please go on. Give me some examples of how you use all the crayons in your daily life."

He told her that he'd learned to say, "Two big beers," in fourteen different languages, that he'd committed to memory interesting trivia about meaningless matters, and that good manners and consideration were without fail reciprocated.

"In the small, wee hours, I'd superglue quarters to sidewalks outside of a busy downtown office buildings. Then I'd pack a lunch and spend the noon hour watching shifty executives trying to surreptitiously pick it up without betraying how cheap they were."

He told about the time he chainsawed the top forks off a sturdy tree, stuck four eye-hole bolts in about 30 feet up, bought about a hundred yards of medical supply tubing and — *voila!* — invited friends to a giant slingshot party where they spent the afternoon bombarding the neighbors with spray-painted potatoes from 500 yards away.

"Once, just for fun, my friends and I got good and drunk and tried to walk through an airport metal detector wearing rented suits of armor. I sent all my Christmas cards out in March so I could ensure I'd be first to issue season's greetings three seasons in advance. Without fail, I always overtipped the underpaid and I did a lot of fun stuff nude in public wearing nothing but my sneakers."

By the time she'd come back for her 23rd visit, she'd collected more than 300 items and a $100,000 advance from a publisher interested in backing her book, "Use All the Crayons! Marty McCrae's Tips on How to Lead a Colorful Life!" The instant book was an instant bestseller, infuriating Buster that Marty'd cavalierly signed away all the rights.

Marty was thrilled and believed leaving a wealthy widow would be more fun than dying alone in the company of one lucky wealthy stranger and Buster. But with the success of the book, Penny Hart immediately gave up her plans to pursue a medical career, moved to Carmel-by-the-Sea in California and married a painter. For the next few years, Marty always remembered her fondly when he received her brightly colored Christmas card each March.

As for marriage, he told Buster, "Well, I guess it's just not meant to be. I suppose I'll die alone. No more marriage proposals for me."

Buster nodded and the next week noted that McCrae was already talking marriage again with a 24-year-old waitress who was perfectly charmed when she heard him say he always overtipped the underpaid. Buster stopped counting the proposals after about the next dozen.

Even at 112, McCrae was still a sucker for girls who whose eyes were as warm and inviting as brim-filled cups of steaming cappuccino.

⁓✳︎⁓

Becky Dudash knew her acting ambitions were kaput when U.S. Vice President Maggie Cashen asked for her autograph. She'd gushed that she'd seen Dudash profiled the night before on one of the top entertainment shows and said she was struck by how much they had in common.

"We both like antiques, we're both are attracted to taller, older men and we both aspired to be soap opera actresses," Cashen said. "And look where we both ended up!"

It had caused a minor stir when Cashen, a chronic gambler, had started skipping state functions in favor of waiting in line to take a chance on McCrae. Her critics included the speaker of the U.S. House of Representatives, the Senate majority leader and the president herself. The Beltway pundits uniformly howled.

"Inappropriate!" they thundered. Headline writers giddily seized on the opportunity to pair Cashen with various manifestations of "Ca$h-in!" She held a press conference to address the controversy and did so head-on.

What would she do if she was in the room when McCrae died?

"I will promptly resign the vice presidency and purchase a lovely villa amidst the flowering bougainvillea somewhere in the Caribbean," she said, holding up a fan of brochures. "I'll spend the remainder of my days sipping pina coladas and anonymously sending bundles of hundred dollar bills to unfortunates I read about in the news."

Are any taxpayer dollars being used to fly you here or to purchase your ticket?

"No, it's all out of my own pocket. My accounts are an open book for you to examine."

Are you among the multitudes who're praying he'll die for you?

"The short answer is no," Cashen said. "Mr. McCrae is a national treasure. We've all seen the stories about his remarkable life, the people he's met, the places he's been and the things he's done. I'm interested in meeting him for my own gratification. I love hearing his stories and look forward to lively conversation with this wonderful man. That being said, he can't live forever. If he's going to die, he might as well do it while I'm on the X."

The press conference came to a sloppy conclusion after Cashen dissolved in a fit of laughter after one reporter asked if she was neglecting any important vice presidential duties by spending so much time waiting in line at the ghoul pool gala.

The criticism all washed away as one-by-one, every major elected official from both parties was snapped waiting in line to see McCrae. Even President Marcia Tender came once, although she did it under the guise of being a gracious host for a group of European diplomats who'd said they were eager to take a chance on McCrae and the mega-millions that beckoned one and all.

Dudash liked Cashen and had voted for the Tender/Cashen ticket in 2076 because of the pair's honesty and progressive natures and because it was the first time in America a party had nominated an avid lesbian and a thrice-divorced free spirit to high office. And she realized things would never be the same for her after Cashen recognized her, called her by name and began making familiar girly talk as her turn with McCrae approached.

Becky had been an out-of-work actress when she got the role of McCrae's nurse. It was supposed to be little more than part-time window dressing, in a role she was supposed to share with two other actresses. But her winning banter with contestants and reporters had made her an overnight sensation and nearly as big a star as McCrae himself. Surveys showed that meeting her was giving contestants just as big a charge as meeting McCrae. Buster and Bolten museum director Vanwig decided to consolidate the role around her. She would be the only nurse. She would live on property and was given the personal fitness center she requested so she could keep in shape for the action roles she hoped would one day soon begin coming her way. In exchange for her commitment, she was given a $500,000 advance and a yearly salary of $1.5 million with a stupendous escalator clause that Buster agreed to only because he remained confident McCrae couldn't possibly make it through Thanksgiving. If securing her cooperation meant promising her money she'd likely never see then Buster was happy to oblige.

She was also free to negotiate her own deals for books, essays, sponsorships and other promotional activities. The lucrative sideline lead to $1 million in contracts in just the first month.

With that kind of money, she threw herself into the role. She began supplementing her Soap Opera Magazine reading with books about actual nursing. Whenever someone asked, and they always did, "Psst, hey, how's he doin'?" Dudash would pull out a chart and say, "His vitals are strong, his outlook good. But, remember, you're dealing with the world's oldest man here. He could go at any second. Why not you and why not now?"

It was just what everyone wanted to hear and no one would have cared that the "chart" was a detailed listing of area take-out restaurants who'd agreed to provide Buster and Marty with free food in exchange for promotional considerations.

She hadn't had a real boyfriend in more than year and recognized she was off the table for as long as McCrae was alive. He was her steady. She spent her every waking hour either with him or thinking about him. Still, she was pleased by the offers of flirty strangers. It gave her hope for a post-McCrae future that she'd find someone fun, loving and interesting — someone, she imagined, like Marty McCrae was about 75 years ago.

She'd read stories about how men and women met and fell in love five seconds at a time during the mundane exchange at turnpike toll booths. It fascinated her. And now she was sensing how that dynamic worked.

Attractive men would come by once a week and flirt with her for 15 minutes as they waited to step into the isolation security chamber before being whisked to the X. There were the normal horny guys who were emboldened by the assured lack of rejection by a captive audience. They would swagger in, ballcaps all cockeyed, hit on her and promise to call if McCrae dropped dead for them. Some she'd never see again. Others became less boastful as she began to recognize them and welcome them back by name.

Then there were the sophisticated Wall Street types who tried to look down their noses at the jackpot and pretend they were doing it just for a lark. She knew they were greedy bastards and, if she had to choose, would have preferred the dinner company of one of the horny jokers.

Then there was George Prince. He was a Tennessee cabinet maker with wavy light brown hair that looked to Dudash like it would shower sawdust if he shook his head like the way wet dogs do. He had a sister in New York who brokered deals for his high-end furniture at various boutique stores that valued his work. He'd been married once. Didn't have kids and one day hoped to find time to play more golf.

It took her about four visits to find out that much about him. Two visits later, she knew he played mandolin in pickup bluegrass bands at the Station Inn in Nashville and that he enjoyed spending time volunteering at a local soup kitchen. She saw him reading a popular biography of abolitionist suffragette Susan B. Anthony and made an instant connection. She was reading it, too.

"You know, because of her," he said, "there'll never be another person who can be described as an abolitionist suffragette. It's a term she wore and worked to render obsolete. That's rare in history. To me, that's a bit of a pity because abolitionist suffragette sounds superhero cool to me."

On his 8th visit he handed her a little carving of Jesus he'd whittled for her. She thought it was beautiful and gossip columnists who'd taken to speculating about her personal life made note that she was getting gifts from a stranger with a Southern accent.

She found herself thinking about him if he hadn't stopped by her toll booth in more than a month.

"You know, he's a really sweet guy," Vice President Cashen told her. "I spent about an hour in line with him just last week. He's got a real crush on you, you know."

She knew.

But, she knew, too, that she already had a boyfriend, one who demanded all her time and all her attention. She loved him. He made her laugh and feel special. But she knew it wouldn't last forever.

Marty McCrae had to die some day.

Everybody did.

DECEMBER 2078

The reporters all had to pay the same $25 per visit as everybody else. And just like everybody else, they got almost 15 minutes and then — *Wheeee!!!* — they were dropped screaming into the darkness and deposited right at the gift shop where they had the opportunity to browse and purchase Excesstival-authorized McCrae caps, t-shirts, key chains and authentic McCrae replica coffins.

The same rules applied to the producers, lighting crews and videographers, which led to many logistical problems each crew person had to wait in line for several hours with his or her gear, set up — it sometimes took teams of two or three to get the job done with some efficiency — and move on. Then the same for the segment producers. Then finally the on-air personalities.

The unions complained that they should be given special consideration because they were acting as promotional agents. Buster balked and said he didn't need their promotions. The union bosses threatened to withhold coverage. Buster said he didn't care one way or the other. The McCrae ghoul pool was a self-perpetuating money printing machine that didn't need the oil of publicity to keep all the parts working

— as long as McCrae's remaining vital internal organs kept functioning.

The dispute was resolved when the union put it to a vote that lost when the membership voted in a landslide to keep covering the event under Buster's existing rules as long as the union kept paying full admission for members who worked out an agreement that they'd split any winnings with dues-paying members.

So the news crews showed up en masse to clog the lines around the holidays with maudlin reports on McCrae's holiday recollections and forecasts. A boomlet of interest erupted when it was revealed that he'd been a life-long fanatic about making and keeping New Year's resolutions.

"It all started back in 1987 when I realized my left hand didn't do a damn thing," he said. "Nothing. It just kind of hung there like a spare long sleeve. Every other part of my body really pitched in and contributed a little bit. Each leg, each ear, each eye — they all helped the team out. But the left arm just didn't do squat. It started pissing me off. The left thumb, especially, was an irksome loafer. It was the only digit out of 10 that didn't even so much as bang the space bar when I typed. When it came to typing, the left thumb never lifted a finger."

So he resolved on that New Year's Eve to use his left hand to drink more. He was naturally right-handed and used his right hand to write, toss a ball and do so many other routine day-to-day actions that he began to realize that the left hand had was becoming a lazy, good-for-nothing loafer. Sure, it couldn't be trusted to toss a dart if a pregnant woman was within eight feet of the cork, but the very least it could do was pick up a mug of beer once in a while.

As it was the holidays, he helpfully suggested reporters headline the story about his resolutions, "A Wonder-ful Life." His life, he said, had been full of wondering.

"I was born with a very restless mind," he said. "I clearly remember standing in the shower during my first marriage. I'd heard Sir Isaac Newton was so brilliant that he'd sit consumed in thought on the edge of his bed for hours unable to move. He was thinking about great theories of physics that would shape intellectual thought for centuries. Me, I was immobilized by things like shampoo."

On days he'd planned for getting haircuts he remembered being lost in contemplation about which was the more fitting shampoo to use. Should he use a splash of his then-wife Val's good stuff or go with the industrial strength generic he doused with near daily?

The reporters seemed to hang on his every word. He imagined himself Solomon on the verge of conveying some universal truth.

So, they wanted to know, what did you do?

Marty let the drama build for two beats. "I grabbed the good stuff and poured out a healthy palmful. I felt honor bound to give the hairs that had served me so well a kind of last meal before I marched them off to their scissored demise. And that was the year I resolved to out of gratitude to treat my hairs better on the days they'd depart."

His life became an annual carnival of novel resolution. One year he'd resolve to eat his meals in reverse with breakfast at night and dinner after waking up and for one year began every day with a rich desert before moving onto things like steak or spaghetti and meatballs and a big bowl of Lucky Charms for the day's last meal, while lunch remained lunch. He felt a surge in productivity the year he gave up reading newspapers or watching the news, figuring he'd read or seen every story humanity had to offer and it was all by now a yawning rerun. One year he vowed to wear only gentleman's chapeaus and no more pedestrian ball caps. He was late everywhere he went the year he took a balloon-tying class and had vowed to tie little purple poodles for every child he passed in the neighborhood. The delays and late appointments wound up costing him a fortune, but it'd all been worth it, he later concluded.

None of his resolutions ever sought to eliminate any of his numerous vices, all of which he enjoyed and nurtured like a garden abundant with weeds. He reveled in drink, being drunk, smoking cigars, gambling, skipping church, swearing at inappropriate times and spending prolific amounts of time in the dubious company of Buddy and Skip, the two loquacious friends who could produce over one six pack of beer more distracting mind manure than a herd of cows could in a rainy month. He would love them forever.

He remembered the summer of the "ALL HONESS STRANJERS WELCOM!" parties as the year he urged Buddy to resolve to be a better speller. It was embarrassing. Buddy'd spent the summer of 1985 passing out posters one week before his famous pig roasts and included directions, phone numbers, times, dates and always on the bottom in big, bold letters, with 75 percent misspellings, "ALL HONESS STRANJERS WELCOM."

During the previous six months, honest strangers had ripped Marty off of three Rolling Stones tapes, $60 in cash and a set of spare golf clubs. He suggested if Buddy was really intent on having these parties he ought to just put "LIARS WELCOME" on the signs. Marty believed it would reduce the chance of misspelling so many simple words and the people who showed up wouldn't have to mislead anyone about their fraudulent intentions.

"It lets people know we're friendly," Buddy said.

"It lets people know we're stupid," Marty said.

The reporters pestered him about what he'd resolve for the year 2078. Buster looked horrified when he said he was resolving to die, so Marty didn't tell that joke anymore. He satisfied their need for punchlines by resolving to stop salting cereal. The novelty that someone still used salt, much less used it on cereal, charmed a society that had long ago become terrified by once common kitchen table things like salt, bread butter and sugar.

Really, his true resolutions had been whittled down to just one. Like this year and every year since the horrific echo of the rifle blast in 2032, he was again resolving to finally come to peace with Buddy's death. Amid the comic carnival of festive resolutions, this one stood out through its sobriety of intention matched with his utter failure to achieve it year after year.

IN DREAMVILLE …

The first group resembled to Marty the tribal counsel panels Jeff Probst used to host on the old "Survivor" reality TV show. Only here in Dreamville, the stakes weren't $1 million and the title of sole survivor. Those were peanuts compared to what was up for grabs in Dreamville.

The stakes in Dreamville were the survival of Marty's eternal soul. He took another big gulp of bourbon.

"Come on in, guys," Buddy said.

With faces like fists, ten of them marched lockstep onto the stage. Recognition made Marty wince. They were most of his ex-wives, the ones that hated him. He was disappointed that he couldn't see the three or four that might have been supportive of him as husband, father, lover or cleverly deceptive bridge partner. He tried to think who, exactly, those women might be, and was stumped. He took another gulp and looked over at Buddy.

This wasn't the Buddy of the "why, Buddy? Why?" days. It was the Buddy he'd met as freshman at Ohio University in Athens, Ohio, where popular t-shirts were emblazoned with things like "You Can't Spell Bourbon Without OU," and "Ohio University: A Fountain of Knowledge Where We Go to Drink." Buddy's hair hung down to his shoulders and was the color and curling volatility of a mud puddle in a hailstorm. At the time, he was still fit and it was a year before the beginnings of a generous midriff combined with a casual posture that always made Marty think his friend would be a really comfortable chair if he were furniture.

"Marty, it's great to see you," Buddy said and Marty could tell it was heartfelt. He wanted to get up and hug his old friend but the deadening inertia of the breast-like blue chair made elevation impossible. "It may not seem like it, but one day, I swear, you're going to die. Your earthly days will come to an end. It happened to me. It'll happen with you. Happens to all of us. It's just a natural part of life."

"It wasn't with you," Marty said and instantly felt sorry he did. The crowd simmered with disapproval and Marty knew he'd been impolite. Buddy didn't seem to mind. Nothing ever bothered Buddy. Well, hardly.

"Well, we're not here to talk about me. This is all about you. We've assembled many of the most pivotal people in your life to tell you to your face what kind of man you've been lo these many years."

Marty looked at the platoon of ex-wives. They looked like they wanted to tear him limb from limb. He took another slug of bourbon. Drunk, he knew he could withstand any torment known to man. Well, except holy matrimony. He'd proven that 16 times with 13 different women.

"First of all," Buddy said, "We're going to hear from some of the women to whom you'd expressed your undying love, to whom you committed before man and God a singular faithfulness that would endure through the ages. Here are a dozen of 'em. Others will have their turns later. Wanna know what you're playin' for? It's the big enchilada."

At this even the donkey stopped chewing and turned around.

"It's heaven or hell, Marty," Buddy said. "What you say here will determine the eternal placement of your very soul. You cool with that?"

Marty thought back. He'd always been vainly certain he was a cinch to make the heavenly cut. He'd been kind to children and old people, never hogged the passing lane for extended periods or sent annoying ALL CAP E-MAILS. Sure, that's setting the heaven bar pretty low, but by modern standards he felt it amounted to near saintly behavior. Now, with it all on the line, he wasn't so sure.

"Well, no, I'm not good with that," Marty said. "Many of these people have an ax to grind. I don't think anyone would want to be judged by a jury of their ex-wives."

"We're all judged by those whom we've loved and left behind. That is our legacy. This, my friend, is yours."

He was taken aback by the hostility he saw on the faces of Valerie, Becky, Judy, Isabella, Guadalupe, Brooke, Carla, and the three Kims.

After some helpful biographical introductions read by Buddy, the women began to speak in turns, in teams and all at once.

Wives 2, 3, 6, 8 and the second and third Kims complained that he was unfaithful. Wives 1, 5, 7, 9 and the first Kim said all he ever thought about was sex, while wives 2, 3 and 6 said he left them starved for affection. Wives 1, 4 through 8, and the first Kim all complained about his laziness and how all he wanted to do on weekends was sit on the couch and watch old John Wayne movies. When wife no. 6, Brooke, said, "And you were always drunk," the other wives all nodded their agreement. Same for when wife no. 7 complained that he'd never done any work around the house.

There was talk about his cheating with waitresses, pastry chefs, factory girls, school crossing guards and at board games like Monopoly. He'd treated badly, they near uniformly agreed, their parents and siblings and he'd joked with tedious redundancy that the only difference between in-laws and outlaws were that outlaws were at least wanted by someone. His first seven wives belittled him for an immaturity that lingered into his 70s when he grudgingly and finally gave up his massive beer can collection he'd tended since the fourth grade. They disparaged his quadrennial efforts to appear as loathsome as possible for the driver's license photo ID session on the belief that if he'd ever get pulled over he'd appear naturally less repugnant to the cop than the guy in the picture did (he'd sworn throughout his life that the ruse had worked well enough to get him bumped from numerous drunken traffic violations).

The seven with whom he'd partnered to conceive 11 children all lambasted him for behaving more like playmates than a father to their needy offspring. Becky, the mother of his twins boys, told how it had always infuriated her when he'd sided with the children and how she'd felt humiliated by his habit of shoving fingers in his ears, closing his eyes and singing, *"I Wish I Was In The Land Of Cotton …"* whenever she tried to reason out an adult discussion with them, a rhetorical habit the children never dropped.

"To this day, those boys still wave those damned Confederate flags in my face whenever I tell them to clean up their room," she fumed. "And they're 37, still living at home and fighting every night over who gets the top bunk!"

Marty was relieved to learn that, at least in Dreamville, neither of the boys had become attorneys.

An internal dispute arose between two of the Kims when the second Kim said he was an unimaginative love maker who left her unsatisfied. The third Kim disagreed and went into a detailed defense of the lewd loverly lengths to which Marty went to please her. She recounted the little house they'd shared near Seal Beach with the rumpus room trampoline and the trapeze he'd spent a weekend affixing to the ceiling that dangled to about 36-inches above their waterbed.

"I'll give you that much, Marty," said Kim III in a near swoon of lusty recollection. "You were an unfaithful and drunken lout of a husband, but in the sack, man, you were Mr. Perfect. You were wild. You really knew how to push my buttons, babe. Yeah, there'll never be another Marty."

Marty was practically beaming until he looked his other nine ex-wives. They looked like they wanted to kill him. And they may have, but Buddy stepped in.

"I think that's enough for now, ladies," he said. "I think what you're saying is Marty was a poor husband, liked to drink, was childish well into his 90s, and disliked tackling any household projects that didn't involve circus equipment. Anything you want to say, Marty?"

He thought about mentioning that he always made a point of trying to cheat on them with older, uglier women because he understood how sensitive women were to men who left wives for younger babes. And, not incidentally, how grateful the older, uglier gals were for the flattering interest he showed them. It was his idea of feminism. His mind flipped through dozens of arguments that had failed during multiple marriages that had also failed and decided a defense ~~would~~ against such a bitter barrage would have been fruitless. So Marty figured he'd surprise them all, smile and just say thanks.

"At one time in my life, each of you did something to make me the happiest man in the world," he said with a heartfelt smile. "I've been so blessed throughout my life to have good friends who mean the world to me. Friends like Buddy, here. But even though my marriages to you did not endure and some of them only last a months and one of them lasted just 8 days — sorry first Kim — there was something about each of them I still treasure. I wasn't cut out to be much of a husband, I guess, or a father. And that's something I regret. But thanks to each of you for some shade of joy you brought to me. My whole life, I loved being in love. And you were among the women I loved most of all. For that, I owe you all so much."

Buddy beamed in precocious admiration. He knew it would work. It did.

There was a simultaneous gal gush — "Ahh!" — from nine of the ex-wives to whom he'd been married 14 separate times. The only one who wasn't moved was Kim II, whom Marty remembered as "Bitter Kim." She'd heard a similar speech shortly after she'd ended her second marriage to Marty and wasn't falling for that one again. But the rest of them, God bless 'em, they gathered around Marty and pulled him out of the breast chair to give him one big hug. And only wives 2, 8 and the first Kim slapped him when he pinched them on the asses. The crowd burst into applause. They were enjoying the show.

Because it was all a dream, Marty couldn't be sure, but he swore he saw the donkey wink.

MARCH 2079

"That's not what I said," Marty said with self-righteous vigor.

"Yes, it is."

"No, I'm certain you're mistaken. I would never have said those words. No way, no how."

"You said them May 11, 2025, to a worldwide satellite television audience nearly 50 years ago. Here, I have the transcript."

Marty lay barefoot on the bed. The toes on his left foot had become so spread out and nimble he was the first person in history capable of giving someone the finger with the foot. He dug his tootsies under the sheets to avoid a scandal.

"Let me see that thing," McCrae said, and testily held out his hand. He may, in fact, have said, "I really think sub-letting about 1,000 acres of the Grand Canyon, just a fraction of the park's total acreage, will accelerate development that could lead to construction of some spectacular golf courses on a site that's grown rather stale for anyone who's been to places like the moon," as contestant Tina Sheridan was claiming. McCrae'd been lost in a long reverie of the past when time ran out and the trap door opened releasing, thankfully, a bulb-headed moron who'd done nothing but stare at McCrae for 15 minutes. He'd hypnotized him, he suspected. He was still in a fog when Sheridan came marching past Buster to confront McCrae.

"I'll be damned," he said, glancing through the sheaf of papers. "I guess constructing a golf course on the Grand Canyon was partly my idea. I'd honestly forgotten it. It was a long time ago. But I'm man enough to admit I was wrong and owe you an apology. It must have seemed like a good idea at the time. But I guess it was a rather stupid thing to say. Sorry. Oh, well. My bad!"

But the apology wasn't enough for Tina. She was the 49-year-old single mother whose dour face looked as if any grin that ever crossed it would be arrested for trespassing. Her hair was dulled by sun-bleached perspiration and a defiant avoidance of things like shampoo. Her brown fingers appeared cracked and calloused from digging in the dirt, and tiny tufts of downy fur poked from her unshaven underarms. This one could be trouble. Buster sensed it, too.

Outraged environmentalists had been coming in en masse to rail at McCrae for the reckless ideas he'd hatched that went on to wreak havoc on Mother Earth, the moon, and several inconsequential nearby planets he'd helped turn into playgrounds little different from places like Myrtle Beach and Ocean City. Sheridan had entered agitated and was building up a lather when she brought up McCrae's involvement constructing an elevator to the top of Mt. Everest under the guise of making it more handicapped accessible. McCrae and his partners reaped a fortune after Tibet approved their plans to build the Top of the World Spa & Casino at the summit of what mountaineers like Sheridan used to regard as the ultimate climbing challenge.

To Buster, it looked like she was going to charge the bed at any minute. "Ma'am?" Buster intervened. "Please obey all posted rules and stand directly on the X." Marty gave Buster a quick nod. This one had him worried, too.

"Did you ever even think of the consequences?" she railed. "Did you ever consider anything besides crass profit?"

"Well, of course I did, but I thought Mt. Everest should be made handicapped accessible. Why should the top of the world be the sole domain of the fanatically fit?"

"Look, bub" — her finger shot the word "bub" out at McCrae like an angry javelin — "I'd trained 10 years to conquer Everest. And then you come along with your, 'Say, wouldn't it be nice if everyone could spend a few minutes at the top of the world?'"

"It seemed like a good idea at the time," Marty said defensively. "Buster, you thought it was a good idea, didn't you?"

"I went five times, boss." Buster normally refused to be drawn into McCrae's conversational entreaties, but the Everest thing, man, Buster thought that was pretty cool.

"But, c'mon! An elevator to the top of Mt. Everest? You and your corporate sponsors deprived us of the ultimate challenge. Ten years I trained. I broke bones in three falls. I survived ice falls, avalanches, carelessly tied ropes, and a freak squall that wiped out an entire expedition of Japanese computer programmers. But I survived it all. Then on May 11, 2036, just as my dreams are in reach, you and your party come dancing out of your vertical chariot and take over the top. They would not even let me through the conga line to get to the summit! And there you were in the center of it all, guzzling champagne. And that disgusting shirt. I'll never forget it. 'Party Naked! 29,035 feet!' Men and women had died on that sacred mountain. It was consecrated with their blood, and there you were dancing on their graves with some cheap whore."

For Marty, that tore it. Sherpa Shirley, as he called her, was not a cheap whore. She'd cost him seventy rupees, six cartons of cigarettes and a yak before she'd agreed to sleep with him. Sure, the Everest Elevator hadn't quite worked out like they thought, but it had been worth a shot. Lots of people were still paying up to $20,000 to ride up and spend the night, enjoy dinner and maybe play some blackjack at the Top of the World Casino. That was less than half of what it would cost to hire a guide and some Sherpas to haul pampered butts up to the top of the mountain. And, no one on the elevator came down with a crippling case of diarrhea — and just try climbing Everest without getting a case of the trots.

"You can't stop progress," he said. "People were getting killed on that mountain. We tried to make it safe for everybody, so everybody could enjoy it. You know, like Disney World!"

The mention of Disney set her off. "You ruined it!" again, she menaced toward McCrae.

"Ma'am, I'm not going to ask you again," Buster warned. "Please remain on the X."

She wasn't listening. "It's a sacrilege and it was all your fault!"

Buster's spry reaction belied his pudding-like physique. On the arm of his chair was an array of buttons. He slammed the red one just as she lunged for him. The button activated the tiny powerful magnets that had been unknowingly inserted in each contestant's shoes as they went through the screening process. The magnets instantly drew her back to the trapdoor and effectively froze her on the X. Just for fun, Buster pressed the green button so she could surge forward, then pressed the red again, snapping her back to the X. He did this about four times, each time instigating fresh fury.

"Stop it! Stop it, you bastards!" she screeched. Both Marty and Buster roared with laughter. It was the first time the magnet magic had been deployed and it was a wonder to behold. He let her get within a foot of Marty before zipping her back to base as the old man nearly doubled over in hysterics. For Buster, the exercise was an unexpected delight.

"You can't fight progress, lady!" Marty hollered. "Next time you go up to Everest, you can stop and get a cheeseburger at the Hooters we're putting up. We're selling franchises. There'll be a wax museum and a Ripley's Believe it or Not. Once they get done with the Cracker Barrel, it'll be just like Pigeon Forge!"

As her time ticked down, she was wobbling and weak kneed, but her feet remained rigid, as as if they'd been immersed in cement. "You've not seen the last of me! I'll get you, you bastards! We'll take this planet back. I swear!"

ding!

And with that, she was gone. The X opened, automatically unsealing the magnetic bond and she dropped out of sight. McCrae scampered over to the trapdoor, leaned down and yelled, "See ya in DollyWood!" just before she was replaced by a new contestant. He gave a satisfied chuckle and said to Buster, "Say, that was an invigorating dust-up. Next time, just let her go a little longer so I can introduce her to Mr. Right." He made a fist of his right hand and ran it into his open left with a loud smack. "I was quite a brawler in my younger days, you know. I could have given her something to really remember me by."

Buster looked at him evenly. "She'd snap your bony little ass in two like a twig."

An earnest theologian with a tumbleweed toupee spent two months pestering Marty and Buster to let him put pop tab receptacles in the lobby for people to donate their pop tabs. He intended to take the piles of pop tabs and donate them to groups that would convert the tiny bits of metal into crucial minutes for sick kids on kidney dialysis machines.

Buster was open to the idea for mercenary reasons. He'd go along with it if for a 20 percent cut of the proceeds. But Marty was adamant. Over his dead body, he said. He was slamming the door of darkness on Pastor Kenneth Truman of the Eternal Sun Church of the Open Door.

"But, pray tell, my child, why would you be opposed to helping sick kids?" Truman asked him.

Marty had tried to be polite around clergy, even though he'd long railed against the dreamy disorganized practitioners of organized religion. But being called "my child" by a youth of 29 snapped his patience.

"First of all, sonny boy, I'm old enough to be your great-great-great grandfather so for God's sake stop calling me your child," Mary said. "Second, you're perpetuating a canard, a lie, a deception. Pop tabs into dialysis minutes represents what Charles Dickens would have called a 'humbug' before we took a perfectly good year-round word and shackled it to a Christmas fable. It is impossible to use those little pop tabs to extend the lives of dialysis patients."

Marty was right. He'd first heard about the ploy in 1985 as a gullible college student when he'd dutifully begun pulling off the tabs from soda pops and beers and putting them in community receptacles in dorms and cafeterias. He'd initially been charmed by the whimsy of the act. He loved the calculus that the more beers he'd drink, the more helpful he could be to less fortunates. So drink he did, always taking pains to remove the can key on top and save them all for worthy disposal. Then, in an moment of uncommon insight, he began to wonder how it was at all possible. Could sick kids really be saved that way? If it the pull top equalled one full minute, wouldn't the whole can equal at least 20 minutes? He checked it out and, as he suspected, it was an urban legend. Like similar myths, he didn't know how it started, why it spread and what the hell happened to all those pop tabs whenever someone showed up with the big receptacles full of the tiny shinies down at the kidney dialysis. He supposed the do-gooder donors were crushed to find that dialysis machines didn't have little slots you could drop the pop tabs in and ring up the minutes the way they did coins in parking meters.

That's why he was furious with Buddy during the summer of 1985. That's when Buddy got busted for drunk driving a "Hands Across America" fundraiser float down Court Street in Athens. Reaching for a cold Busch beer, he'd rear-ended an AIDS Awareness float which for symbolical symmetry rear-ended the "Sinner's Repent!" float sponsored by fundamentalists from the local Church of Christ. The church float then crashed into a Court Street Tavern

Association float that featured a giant beer mug that had sorority girls blowing bubbles out of the foam and into the crowd. The parade ended as police swooped in to sort out the wreckage. Four were treated and released at the local hospital, Buddy was cuffed and hauled away and the parade organizer was chastised for organizing the floats in way that could lead to such ironic mayhem.

For community service, the court agreed to let Buddy spearhead a fundraising drive that would oversee the collection of pull top tabs. It was a mission Buddy undertook with startling gusto. First he found a perfectly pathetic looking patient, Timmy Oates, to plaster all over the receptacles that began blooming all over the campus. They were in bars, coffee shops and spaced like sentries along the sloping promenades at the Convocation Center. News articles in the morning Post fostered a sense of civic pride in donating as many pop tabs as possible and the Athens Tavern Association, the police and the hospital emergency room each reported healthy surges in student traffic as civic-minded young men and women outdid one another to drink the most beers and save the most minutes.

And Buddy became Prince of the Pop tabs. He was celebrated across campus for his philanthropic endeavors. It irritated Marty because it cut into his bar time with the best drinking buddy he'd ever know.

Worse for Marty was how it seemed to swamp even Buddy's "ALL HONESS STRANJERS WELCOM" parties. The pop tab drives had become the singular focus of the parties. It had become like a cult. Buddy, as always, was reminding anyone drinking canned refreshments to put the pull-off tabs in a five-gallon drum near the cooler marked with thick black magic marker in more of his chicken dance scribble: "Yer pull taps can save lives. Each one can be kunverted to 1 minnet on a kidney mashine. May God Bless You, Buddy Allman."

A college graduate, Buddy couldn't spell but he sure could inspire. Buses of honess stranjers bearing crates of pop tabs would show up in the field east of town not far from where Buddy'd sworn the past year he'd been abducted by aliens.

He'd gotten drunk, passed out and revived in a cow field surrounded by grazing heifers. He spent the next week telling everyone who'd listen that he'd been picked up and probed by an alien spaceship.

"They probed me with this big silver drill right up the ass," he said. "Oh, man, did it hurt. And then, I swear, they put a chip in my butt. Lookee here ..."

More people saw Buddy's bare ass that week than during the weekend he'd spent at the Sunny Recline Naturalist Camp and Retreat, the illicit Hocking Hills nudie campground Buddy where Buddy and Skip went for yearly frolics. He'd drop his drawers and brazenly display a big, red welt everyone agreed was a nasty spider bite. Everyone but Buddy, who honestly believed it was an alien monitoring device, one that itched any time a low pressure system came up out of the Ohio Valley.

To Marty in recollection, the whole summer of '85 seemed like he'd been involved in a particularly odd cult. Devotees would achieve their heavenly aims only through drinking as much canned beer as they could consume. He didn't know whatever happened to the mountains of pop tabs Buddy'd collected that summer, if they were ever disposed of properly or if little Timmy Oates or any other kidney dialysis patient enjoyed even an extra minute due to Buddy's soulful diligence.

But he knew it was all nonsense. And that's what he told Pastor Ken.

"I won't help you perpetuate a foolish myth," Marty said. "Instead, why don't you lead your flock into the ghettos and help one family get sober and stay intact. That's a worthy goal."

But Pastor Ken would not be dissuaded. He and the Church of the Open Door became a de facto church of the open can. The sound of beer cans opening — *Ka-ploosh!* — became as common as shouted *"Amens!"* Attendance shot up and it became the church of choice for backsliders who needed some heavenly hair of the dog.

Marty could only shake his head and wonder about all those pop tabs and why Buddy, a man who'd tried so hard to save others in the end couldn't save himself.

APRIL 2077

Marty was always an optimist who when he found a magic marker in an empty room still tried to use it to turn things like chairs into gold.

Such enduring human cheerfulness was evident throughout the eighth floor of the Bolten where museum exhibits lavished attention on Marty's crackpot inventions and the social crusades he'd inspired. Admittance was included in the $25 ghoul pool tickets. Many customers chose to linger for hours among the displays before lining up to wait their turn to say a friendly hello to Marty and a fast prayer that he'd quickly drop dead for them.

There were pictures of Marty base-jumping from atop at the pyramids at Giza, skateboarding down the Great Wall of China, playing near-zero gravity lunar golf deep in the Sea of Tranquility. Left unmentioned was that most of pictures had been snapped by Will Ponce and that the junkets were his splurges, as well. Only a few pictures in the entire museum even included images of Ponce. He had a zipper-thin physique and a crew cut fringe of red hair and always looked to Marty like a No. 2 pencil with a pristine eraser on the top. He carried his entire frame with an erect, stiff spine like the kind you'd find on new Bibles. He smiled often even though Marty'd told him his abnormally long teeth looked like the front of a surf shop run by potheads who left row of bleached boards out in the sun too long. He was the most relentless capitalist Marty'd ever known..

Historians and industry experts were complimentary about the accuracy of the displays. He was correctly given credit for being the first to seize on the idea that cell phones could be used to cure the cancers they caused, and criticized for failing to see that cell phone liposuctions would render the devices incapable of either saving lives or being used to order pizza. A rudimentary model of the machine that allowed people to fax leftovers to the needy was displayed and much admired for its role in helping mitigate global starvation.

There was much praise of his industry-saving idea to build the technology that started with edible newspapers and soon spread to everything from edible plates to edible vending machines

"I have seen the future and it is slathered in ketchup," was the quoted headline. It's what McCrae'd said in 2017 when he applied the technology used when baking savant Douglas Stewart was on November 3, 2003, issued U.S. patent no. 6,652,897. Stewart had developed the popular compound that allowed people to print edible pictures on birthday cakes. Marty had always been an avid newspaper reader and was saddened to see the decline of his daily read. He foresaw the solution to an industry plagued with job losses, vanishing readers and generations who simply didn't care was really a meat 'n' potatoes issue.

The display copy read: "McCrae reasoned that most of our urgent problems could be solved if more of our everyday manufactured items could be consumed instead of being trucked to landfills. He said, 'Think how much waste would be eliminated if, say, after you've eaten a bag of potato chips you could chew up the bag and digest it. Make it mint flavored and heart-healthy and the busy bodies at the American Medical Association would probably recommend it for kids."

Soon, resourceful manufacturers were replacing once ubiquitous plastic bottles with containers made out of pretzel-like substances that were safe to consume as the liquids got lower, much along the lines of ice cream cones and scoops of mint chocolate chip. The natural progression was that vending machine made out of beef jerky were stocking cans made of pretzels that held sodas. The only things that couldn't be consumed were the little metal pop tabs used to open the cans. Those were preserved because many people still persisted in saving them to donate to children who needed precious minutes on kidney dialysis machines.

But it was the use of edible newspapers that was truly groundbreaking. McCrae'd perfected Stewart's technique of printing pictures and lacquering them atop birthday cakes and applied it to newsprint. Stewart's inspiration was that the paper he made was firm enough to be printed on in a standard printer, yet dissolved quickly when brought in contact with moist frosting. It was perfectly safe. And on a cake, just plain cool.

Marty'd concluded there was no better or more practical application than having the same technology devoted to newspapers, a dirty, tree-consuming business if there ever was one. He envisioned mountains of waste that could be eliminated. He thought how helpful it would be to busy executives if they could read a page of the Wall Street Journal and then just eat the page bite by bite the way they would a salad.

It revolutionized newspapers and food writers enjoyed a more elevated position in the newsroom. Instead of being the butt of jokes from the pomposity peacocks dominating the hard news, the food editor would be the one who'd daily decide what it meant for a family newspaper to be truly tasteful.

One screen in the display showed a matronly food editor discussing that day's paper: "All right, there's a big doubleheader at the ballpark today so flavor the sports pages with kosher hot dogs and mustard,' she said. "The front page story about salmonella should taste like salsa because readers aren't going to be getting any of that for a while. And we're running a blowhard opinion piece from Stan, the business editor, about how he correctly predicted the current troubles when everyone said he was nuts. Have that taste like crow."

That was followed by a clip of a much-younger Marty saying, "The newspaper industry has been dying for years and I know they'll resist my ideas. They're stubborn. But I think they'll eventually agree I've offered a perfectly sensible solution to save their jobs. If they choose to ignore it, well, let them eat cake."

A wall detailing many of the social movements he'd inspired and led teemed with interest. It was where he'd enjoyed his most significant impact.

He in the early 21st century became alarmed to learn of the existence of what was then known as The Great Pacific Garbage Patch, a floating island of disgusting flotsam twice the size of Texas. He knew cleaning it up would be futile. So Marty decided the solution was to colonize the floating trash patch. Rather than disparaging the massive plastic islands that were killing earth's marine life, he suggested promoting it as posh island living, the epitome of modern chic.

And it was a huge hit. It became the template for dealing with overwhelming environmental problems by applying vast swaths of industrial make-up and turning waste into wonder.

Then there was the vanity Zip Code plan that bailed out the U.S. Post Office in 2015. As his own dear mother had begun to age he sought to simplify her life. He got rid of her computer, her microwave and the TV remote that had the 54 confusing buttons that did the job of what three would do (on/off, volume and channel arrows). The remote infuriated him most because he remembered all the times he saw this bright and otherwise capable woman staring at it the way he figured the ancients must have stared at a solar eclipse. He immediately began searching for ways to simplify her entire world.

The journey led him to Newton Falls, Ohio, 44444. It was, he figured, the easiest zip code in the entire U.S. to recall and he urged his mother to move there. He'd considered Schenectady, New York, 12345. Of course, then she'd forever be stuck spelling Schenectady and that would never do. It began to dawn on him that few of the nation's zip codes made any promotional sense.

Why was Las Vegas 89123, a lousy fold 'em of a zip code if ever there was one, when it ought to have a numeric combo that resonated with gamblers? Why wasn't Bond,

Colorado, 00007? It could use the slogan, "Double Oh, Double Oh 7, Bond, Colorado: Licensed to Deliver." He began to wonder how much Philadelphia would pay to liberate 01776 from North Sudbury, Massachusetts. Philly, after all, is the birthplace of the greatest nation in the world and 01776 would be a constant mail reminder of that proud history. Why surrender it to North Sudbury which gave the nation what? Geographic balance to South Sudbury?

The display showed a clip of Marty saying that America was so numerically obsessed that it shelled out precious dollars for vanity license plates, and fretted whenever the fickle phone company threatened to bump people from familiar urban area codes. "I think for the good of the nation, it's time we extend that obsession to the humble zip code. I think it's time the government begin selling zip codes to communities that stand to profit from the panache. I pitched the idea to officials at the postal service and do you want to guess how much interest I got from those bureaucrats? That's right. Zip."

The clip reported that Marty remained undaunted. He began targeting local civic leaders who saw promise in the McCrae's vanity zip code plan. A bidding war between rocket centers in Houston and Cape Kennedy was launched over who was more deserving of the count-down zipper 54321. Las Vegas folded on 89123 and offered $7,777,777.77 to be given the unused winner of a zip code 77777.

He conspired with creative historical promoters in Salem, Massachusetts, to cast spells on postal officials to free them the clumsy and pointless postal designation 01970 and cash in on its witch-hunting history by branding the local post office with the mark of the postal beast, 00666?

Soon, municipalities around the country began paying tens of thousands of dollars for zips with zing. Politicians soon climbed on board and assured Zone Improvement Plan (the original name bestowed in 1944 by postal employee Robert Moon) would be amended. Money flowed in and the program forestalled by seven years the archaic demise of the once venerable institution. Still, the vanity zip codes McCrae initiated persist as quaint promotional tools by communities around the country.

More controversial was his plan that called for lit cars for lit drivers. In 2019, everyone had finally concluded the war on drugs had been history's biggest waste of time, money and energy because people, ever after more than 40 years, still really adored drugs and drinking.

News footage showed him testifying before Congress and in high dudgeon announcing, "You can threaten people with public shame, enormous fines and even jail time and — cheers! — they're still going to get drunk or drugged and, God help us, they're going to drive. And it happens in all walks of life, not just with scum of the earth lowlifes that I call my friends. It happens with powerful politicians, soccer moms, church choir directors, school teachers and successful men and women with much to lose. At some point in many otherwise productive and law-abiding lives, scores of people fail to find solace in religion, family or even hundreds of channels of hi-def diversion and say, to heck with it, *"I'm going to Dizzyland!"*

And, more often than not, they were driving to get there. No deterrents worked. By 2025, the legal limit for driving was .02. It had fallen from .12 in just 30 years while the grim drunk driving statistics remained flat. All it did was enrich scores of hack lawyers and made miserable many otherwise upstanding citizens who were guilty of little more than driving while giddy.

Marty felt what was needed was an alternative that would allow police officers and the public to recognize the problem drinkers and either arrest them or just get the hell out of their way. He proposed lit cars as a solution. Cars would need to be fitted with sensors that automatically detect just how much alcohol a driver had consumed. If a driver is being responsible, the car would appear normal.

"If, say, the driver had just lost a long beer chugging game of quarters, then the entire car would glow in an alarming shade of red. This would be helpful on so many levels because the police can't be everywhere at once. But if I were driving my family to church and saw a menacing Mustang glowing red and barreling down the highway, I'd know to pull over to a safe distance and let the driver pass."

He said people who were comfortable with narcing on strangers could even call 911. But the roving alert would be sufficient to clear the road when a drunk approached. It would reduce to near zero the sad collateral damage inflicted by drunks who then may be in for a hard lesson when things like trees and telephone polls fail to take sensible precautions upon their approach.

"Future technological tweaks could include other angry shades, say purple, that indicate when the driver was in a crabby mood and prone to road rage. Because we cannot change human nature. People are still going to get angry and they're still going to get drunk and drive."

Congress passed the legislation and it was signed into law. It was a huge success in lowering fatalities and police were thrilled with the assist. Less successful was Marty's efforts to save people who he felt went though life way too sober.

Guests spent hours reveling in the displays, but few ever bothered to venture clear to the back where a small plaque noted that the exhibit was sponsored by a generous donation provided by the Acme Pharmaceuticals Foundation, the conglomerate responsible for many of the most popular legal drugs. A small picture showed Marty and Acme founder Will Ponce arm in arm in flashy Tommy Bahama shirts circa 1992. Not noted was the picture was taken when the pair had made a small fortune selling illegal drugs that put people in euphoric states of mind, a crime for which Ponce spent four years in federal prison before being freed to make an enormous fortune selling legal drugs that did the same thing.

Also unmentioned on the small copper plaque was the fact that Ponce had been lost in space and presumed dead since 2065.

⌒〰〰〰〰⌒

It was the height of the holy season and prayers of the faithful were becoming a bit more feverish. Jesus Christ died for them, they'd been assured. Why the hell wouldn't Marty McCrae? Sure the thought of eternal salvation was a bountiful balm in a world that was not made for sissies. But spirituality aside, wouldn't the $68 million already racked up on the tote board provide plenty of soulful solace?

Of course it would. So the righteous reasoned praying for the death of one used up old backslider wouldn't offend the Almighty. It wasn't very Christian of them, they understood, but really he was very old, wouldn't shut up and was deliberate in trying to time his loudest farts to coincide with their prayerful "Amens." They just knew he did.

And they were right.

It drove Buster crazy cause he could always see it coming. The petitioner would wind down the prayer and he'd see Marty's eyes get an evil gleam. Then with devastating timing, he'd hear an "Amen!" masked with gas.

But Marty couldn't help it. He liked to talk, liked to joke and was bound to fart. The flatulence, too, leavened the heft of all those grave prayers with their implicit recognition that the great-intergalactic traveler had one final destination still to be determined.

Skip had talked more about heaven and hell than any man he'd ever known. And he could be precise on the topic: "If heaven's not hot tubs filled with horny, naked, harp-strumming supermodels then we all ought to start looking around for a suggestion box."

Marty always liked the horny, naked supermodel aspects of that one. It was Skip's bedrock hope for any afterlife worthy of eternity. But as a devotee of variety, it would have become too repetitious for Marty. He was sure sex for eternity, even great sex, would become tedious. Not to Skip, and he was adamant. There had to be hot tubs. They had to be filled with bona fide supermodels who had to be naked and they had to be horny. He wanted them strumming harps for the sake of heavenly atmosphere. Marty would postulate that he might want to ~~have~~ enjoy accomplishing sex with a homely fiddler who resisted all his urgings. But Skip would have none of that and wouldn't even entertain Marty's contention that every once in an eternity or two he'd like to stop having sex, put on a robe and talk to dead presidents.

"See, I'd love to spend the Happy Hour with Lincoln, George Washington, FDR and even Nixon who I'll bet is a riot when he's drunk," Marty said. "And John Wayne. You gotta love the Duke. And I'd really love to talk to Jesus. Who wouldn't? He's the man. Well, the Son of The Man to be precise, but that's sort of splitting hairs. The problem is I'm sure He's pretty busy in heaven. It's probably, 'You want a better apartment? You'll have to see Jesus. Oh, you want to send your spirit to Earth to haunt your ex-wife? Only Jesus can grant that request.' It'd probably be pretty hard to get any real face-time with Jesus."

Once Marty could wrestle him out of the heavenly hot tubs, Skip did have some creative observations about what he called the mundanities of heaven and hell.

"In heaven," he said, "there will be no war. No loneliness. No disease. No Adam Sandler. And hell will be hell. It will be endless torment. Pain. Isolation. And everybody will get stuck with at least one really bad roommate, and by bad I'm talking about someone like Hitler."

Skip even broke it down to breakfast cereals. "In heaven," he said, "there will be no loathsome frosted toasted oats in the boxes of Lucky Charms. It'll just be Lucky Charms."

Marty just loved this. He'd for years devote nearly 75 percent of his time spent eating a bowl of Lucky Charms to hunting down the brown, tasteless oats with his spoon and getting them out of the way so he could indulge in a candy feast of crunchy marshmallows. Thinking he could wake up everyday and pour a big bowl full of the colorful little charms — to hell with nutrition! — seemed incentive enough to lead a better life.

"And if that's not enough," Skip said, "hell will be a place where all the boogers smell really, really bad and everyone will fight over the last box of nearly empty Kleenex. Go on and think about that. Our mortal boogers give off no discernible odor. In hell, the damned endure eternity with awful smelling nasal debris constantly assaulting the organ devoted to detecting scent. It's a kind of torture that would give Marquis de Sade the warm and fuzzy feelings people like you and I get when we watch movies like 'E.T.'"

Marty at the time was raising an six-year-old daughter with the second Kim. He remembered 8 being the golden age of boogerdom. It was not uncommon for him to walk into the living room and see three or four darling girls with their digits jammed so far up their noses that you worry one might embed a fingernail in their cerebral cortex. He knew it was his duty as a parent to stigmatize this behavior. Stop it! Gross! Bad! But his heart just wasn't in it. If he'd purchased his nose from a department store, he'd have contacted a cheap lawyer about suing the manufacturer under some kind of olfactory lemon law.

The nose, Marty felt, was the gateway to herding delightful aromas into our senses (good), but it round-the-clock produced excesses of gross wastes (bad). If given the option, he swore he'd never inhale another whiff of a fragrant rose or some aromatic soup if he could simply do without ever having to worry about something disgusting dangling from the bullseye focal point of his face. It's just wasn't worth it.

He was always surprised there'd never been a plastic surgery breakthrough procedure that allowed everyone to, in the privacy of our bathrooms, efficiently and sanitarily remove and dispose our nasal wastes the without the indignity of having to shove fingers deep up their faces.

"It should be more like removing lint from the dryer screen," he said, something he always got a little domestic kick out of doing.

He hoped Skip was in heaven and that he was just then enjoying time in hot tubs full of horny, naked, harp-strumming supermodels, and that if he did get hungry the Lucky Charms were within reach and he didn't have far to reach something else that was magically delicious.

JUNE 2079

Marty was fascinated that people everywhere had begun having scannable bar codes implanted in their foreheads so anyone with a cell phone could quickly and anonymously discern names, astrological signs, political dispositions, cereal preferences and the current level of sexual arousal of perfect strangers.

A bright-eyed blonde whose recent fashionable surgeries had transformed her into a shape that reminded Marty of an inverted country gentleman's guitar was telling him all about it.

"Oh, yeah," she said. "Everyone's doing it. It'll finally break down all the artificial barriers that have for so long kept people from finding their soul mates. It's going to change everything."

Marty inhaled deeply in the hopes it would help him appear sagacious. Really, he could tell she was wearing the most intoxicating perfume, Opium, and the fragrance was stirring the distant recollection of his last erection from way back in about 2052. If he could coax a woodie up he swore he was going to show it off to the young lady who'd introduced herself as Gretchen from Albuquerque. He was smitten with her and her generous application of Opium and he told her so.

"And that's why it makes it so difficult for me to inform you that people are still going to have a tough time getting laid," he said. "Not you, Gretchen. You could probably have any man you want. Just not the way you want. I'm so far removed from the horny dating scene that I should be restricted from ever commenting upon it. Yet the topic is irresistible to veteran social observers like me."

Marty told her how everywhere he'd looked all his life he'd seen loneliness, divorce, heartbreak and longing. Much of the social networking designed to facilitate getting together instead foiled heartfelt connections. A young couple would make friendly small talk and exchange coordinates. But then the instant they walked away from one another each was searching their phones to glean what they could from the web. Many once promising relationships were snuffed out when a search indicated one of the besotted prospects had included participation in a nerdy Star Trek Facebook group thus ensuring a cold, texted break up message was quick to follow.

"That's why I'm fearful of the folly that contends there's any way to get two people together that doesn't involve the introduction of lots and lots of liquor, which is how I wound up married to more than a dozen lovely women to whom I'd promised everlasting fidelity and enduring sobriety lo these many years. See, I believe sobriety is a major obstacle to any happiness and that judicious amounts of alcohol are a necessary lubricant to an any enduring marriage."

As he rambled on and on he kept thinking of Gretchen in the nude holding a feather duster. She reminded him of a girl he remembered as Back Alley Sally from York, Pennsylvania, the snack food manufacturing capital of the world. Marty'd met her during a 2019 golf weekend in the town he liked to call The Nation's Waist Basket because of all the gut-expanding junk it produced. He led Sally to his hotel room where she persuaded him to strip nude and let her tie him to the bed. She seductively blindfolded him and said she'd was going to go steal a feather duster off the nearby maid cart outside. Thirty minutes later the door opened and the scent of Opium wafted in like a gust from a fragrant tornado. What followed was more than two hours of spectacular sex with Marty impulsively proposing marriage after every orgasm. Then the blindfold slipped off and Marty was shocked to see, not Sally, but Lourdes, a homely and near toothless Honduran woman, smiling down on him as she rode his rod. Sally, whom he never saw again, had thoughtfully paid Lourdes, the migrant hotel maid, $250 from the $2,000 she'd stolen from his wallet, handed her a feather duster, and told her to show Marty a good time as sort of a parting gift. It was very sporting of her, he thought.

Marty got Lourdes to untie him, thanked her with passionless kiss on the cheek, got dressed and flew to Honduras where he met and married for three weeks his fifth wife, Guadalupe. Now at age 114, he didn't remember anything about the marriage, but he never forgot about Lourdes, her feather duster, and the virile surge he felt anytime he got a whiff of Opium.

But Gretchen kept talking and his erection proved elusive. He was compelled to engage her in conversation and forsake ambitious thoughts of an ancient erection.

"Honey," he said, "I've tried all that. I remember when an app appeared that promised to help us pinpoint with GPS accuracy the exact location of Mr. and Ms. Right. Know what that meant? It meant I was soon hearing the lovelorn lament from young ladies like yourself that said" — and here he affected a high-pitched mocking sweetheart's voice — "'Yes, he was handsome, wants kids, has nice hair, is a libertarian, likes pina coladas and getting caught in the rain and, yes, he is cuckoo for Cocoa Puffs, but, oh, well, his eyes just aren't the precise shade of robin egg shell blue I'm looking for in a mate. Maybe something better will come along.'

"See, with every advance in social media, the infernal pickiness quotient rises ever higher. The more you know about any average guy, the less desirable he's bound to become to those of you looking for suitable mates, not to mention countless prospective employers.

"So what would you advise me to do?" Gretchen asked. He told her to do like he always was always advising single men to do: Lower their standards, find a suitable mate, ply them with liquor and get down to matrimonial business before technological advances renders everyone undesirable before anyone even opens their mouths.

"Soon, and you can count on it, the technology that's supposed to bring us together will ensure none of us ever wants to get near one another."

She smiled at him with a sweetness that made him wish he could jump in a shower and wash about 80 years off his life. She was so beautiful and open hearted he knew he'd have done anything to have her for just one night, just one everlasting memory.

"Will you do me a favor?" he asked."I'd love to," she said.

"You have just 20 seconds left. Will you reach in your purse and give yourself a divine blast of Opium, please? The fragrance provokes special memories for me."

She did as he asked and again she smiled. She said nothing as the trap door whooshed open as the lovelorn and ever hopeful Gretchen gave way to gravity leaving behind a haunting Opium ghost hanging in the air.

It pleased Marty in ways that Buster could not fathom that Gretchen was replaced by a toothless Honduran domestic who'd saved up her money to take a chance that Marty would expire and enrich herself and her family back in Tegucigalpa. Marty could just inhale the Opium and marvel at life's nimble little symmetries.

⸺✦⸺

The summer sun was just rising when the conveyor belt whisked U.S. Federal Marshal Marshall Palley III to the X before Marty's bed. "Martin Jacob McCrae," he snarled with feral contempt.

Palley was built like a fire hydrant on human growth hormones. He was squat, ugly and Marty always felt a canine urge to urinate all over him the instant he spied his distinctive shape. It had been that way for three generations. These Marshalls were not Marty's pallies. Marty reached for a bedside glass of water and was surprised to see his hand shaking enough to rattle the ice like an alarm on a lie detector. He'd been lying to Palley, his allies and ancestors for so long it had become habit.

His grandfather, Athens County District Attorney Marshal Palley Sr., had arrested him and Will, Buddy and Skip in 1992 for the manufacture, distribution and sale of marijuana and other narcotics. Will had persuaded the three of them to help him cultivate a state-of-the-art dope farm about 20 miles south of town. Marty was correctly convinced it would all end in jail time. The notion didn't bother him one bit. He'd been between jobs and later in trial testified his getting stoned was for purely philosophical reasons.

"I believe," he'd said under oath, "those of us who work in places that don't drug test have a social responsibility to test drugs on behalf of those who for occupational reasons can not. I predict marijuana will be approved throughout America for medicinal reasons in 20 years and legalized for recreational use 5 years later. You're on the wrong side of history, your honor."

Ponce needed no such philosophical scaffolding to promote drug usage. He just did it strictly for the money. And he'd made mountains of it. It was the most prolific dope farm east of the Mississippi. It had irrigation, molecular soil testing, retractable sun screener canopies and boxes and boxes of red Christmas ornaments he'd hang on the dope limbs to confuse helicopter narcotic detectives into thinking that the dope was actually rows and rows of thriving tomato plants.

It had worked for nearly three years until Pally Sr. brought down the entire operation in a daring midnight raid that involved evading a host of deadly booby traps, guard dogs, primitive human motion detectors, 20 remote security cameras and the soundly slobber sleeping McCrae snoozing on point in the command center guard post.

None of them seemed to begrudge Marty's tactical failing. Hell, they didn't begrudge much of anything in those days when each spent more time stoned than the heads on Easter Island. Even Ponce didn't mind. He enjoyed the arrest and eventual incarceration as much as anyone. In fact, it was immortalized as a rip-roaring good time. In his excitement, Palley Sr. had forgotten to designate anyone to frisk the suspects for drugs and the four of them got stoned immaculate in the back of the paddy wagon. No one was scared. No one cared. And they knew Will had piles of cash buried around the countryside and would eventually spring for really great party when the illegalities were all disposed of to the satisfaction of the courts.

Besides, Marty was convinced every man ought to do at least a stretch to jail just to see what it was like. He was looking forward to using the time to catch up on all the reading he hadn't done in college when he instead of studying he was farming marijuana and smoking the harvest. It helped him truly relate to the late Lord Babington Macaulay's great quote: "I'd rather be a poor man confined to a garret with plenty of books than a king who didn't love to read." Thanks to jail, recreational reading became a more favored pastime than even getting high. He became the kind of voracious and life-long reader who, if given a choice, would rather sacrifice his driver's license than his library card. He enjoyed it so much he often contemplated petty crime when he couldn't find sufficient solitude to read.

Buddy and Skip didn't care either. They agreed with Marty that every young man should do some time in jail the way their fathers, members of the Greatest Generation, did time in military service in the cause of liberty.

Will was a different matter. Jail had made him more restless than a Wall Street trader stuck between the bells. He was a confusing tangle of ambitions who constantly did things to earn feathers in his cap, but his whole life avoided wearing caps with feathers in them. His ultra-competitive nature manifested itself in that he'd want to win at everything, but also prove he cared less about winning than anyone else. He craved riches and respect, yet thoroughly enjoyed bumming around with Marty, Buddy and Skip, a trio of who forever lacked cash or respect. Their associations with Will, however, eventually led to plenty of both.

It was early on that Will learned that the surest way to wealth in America was through selling drugs. It took getting busted by Palley the First for him to learn just which kind of drugs.

"It's been a long, long time, Martin," said Palley the Third. "Too long, perhaps."

"Yes, it has Junior Junior, yes it has," Marty said. He'd called Marshal Marshall Palley II by the name of Junior and it seemed fitting to continue the insult when the family handed down the stodgy name to yet a third generation. That meant to Marty, Marshal Marshall Palley III was always simply, "Junior Junior."

"It's been since 2065, to be precise," Marty said. "That's back when you were pestering me for clues about the disappearance of Ponce. I told you then what I'll tell you know: I don't know what happened to him. I don't know where he buried his money. And I don't know what the secret ingredient he needed to perfect the formula he was working on that he thought would lead to eternal life."

Palley III shook his head making the veins on his dense neck look to Marty like a straws trying to stir a really thick milkshake. "I don't believe you, Martin. You guys were best friends. You'd shared jail cells, golf courses and, if I'm not mistaken, your sixth and his third wives."

Then that was it. Junior Junior. settled into a sullen silence.

It was all true, Marty knew. In many non-sexual ways, he and Will had always been like one of those perfect couples. They fulfilled vacancies in one another the way a successful husband and wife team did. Oddly, it was the only situation where that had worked for Marty out of more than a dozen matrimonial attempts.

They meshed. Marty was an idea guy, a visionary. He saw clean, shiny scalps and wondered why there weren't luscious hair farms for bald men to harvest. When it became clear that cell phones were causing cancer, he wondered why cell phones couldn't come with a cancer curing app to cure all the cancers they caused. He'd be watching the news and see starving children while he was eating at a diner where piles of uneaten food were pushed from plates into the trash to rot. It appalled him.

"You know," he'd say to Will, "the guy that invents a machine that allows us to fax leftovers to starving children is going to get box seats in heaven."

Will would hear that and think the guy who invents a machine that allows diners to fax leftovers to starving children was also going to make a fortune.

So that's just what Will would do.

"Where there's a Will, there's a way!" he'd always say. He was as prolific with patents as Marty was with crackpot ideas. They made a good team. Will sifted through the ideas Marty was always spouting and launched products and innovations that would earn him billions. Marty got to enjoy all the fruits of Will's lifestyle — luxury travel, golf, fine dining, the sumptuous company of refined lovelies — and he never saw a bill. He was allowed to enjoy one of the greatest lives in the history of living simply for being a good friend. Marty knew this and it pleased him more than say if he'd earned the right through the sweat of his own brow. He considered being a friend worthy of such a lavish treatment a great accomplishment.

"Many people earn fabulous privilege through hard work and intelligence," he' say. "I earned it by being a really sweet guy."

It was a statement Will'd never dispute. He considered Marty's friendship an asset and once sought to have him declared tax deductible. It was one of the few shrewd ideas that failed.

Will's success in engineering legal drugs made him among the richest men on the planet. He had seven homes on three continents and a lunar condo on the rim of the Sea of Tranquility when he disappeared.

Marty had for most of his life been a scratch handicap who'd earned a tax-free fortune as a premier golf hustler who never missed Happy Hour and liked to brag that the only substantive words he'd ever heard from a single tax attorney were amounted to, "And just how much do I owe you, Marty?"

Will owned a building in Manassas, Virginia, where 25 of them worked on nothing but the life and legacy of Ponce's Acme Inc., a vast conglomerate which included an Acme Inc. division that manufacture actual Acme ink.

And, for the most part, both of them could enjoy the respective pursuits thanks to lots and lots of drugs. For that he had Marshal Marshall Pally Senior Sr. to thank. Because it all went back to that very first bust in 1992.

The fable'd been handed down generation after generation in Palley family lore in what came to be known as the "Poncey Scheme." Marty could tell it was consuming Palley as he did nothing but glare at him for minute after minute as if he could stare him death. He'd survived the gunshot wounds of jealous lovers, volcanic eruptions and vicious outbreaks of Hepatitis C through Hepatitis N. But now he feared he was going to be done in by a silence so still it was creeping him out.

"If you think I'm going to die for you in the next 10 or so minutes by just staring at me," Marty said, "you're nuts."

"It wouldn't be the first family fortune you cheated the Palleys out of!"

Junior Junior continued to silently seethe at Marty for the duration of his time before dropping out of sight. Marty was relieved to see him go and fearful he'd return, which he would. Palley'd considered this a scouting mission. He'd be back again and again and again, 249 more times, in fact. Each time incrementally adding to an undetectable toxic stew he'd specially designed from his grandfather's confiscated contraband.

The first visit had been a success. Marshaling and associated detective work had given the Palleys necessary insights into how elaborate detection systems worked, much like the one used to protect McCrae from all the common poisons and bugs that could be smuggled in to slay him for base monetary purposes.

But the system in the Bolten was flawed in that it failed to account for an accumulation of menace, the kind Palley knew he could smuggle in at will. As he scooted down the Death Chute and landed on the sidewalk, he felt a self-righteous flush of intellect that his primary motivation wasn't petty revenge.

No, it was all about the money.

Killing McCrae was just icing on the cake.

IN DREAMVILLE …

Marty had to squint through the smoke at the handsome young couple approaching the stage. They were an attractive pair. He came to that vain conclusion because he sensed a strong resemblance. Both of them in their late 40s but looking maybe 10 years younger, he was pleased to think they might be two of the grandchildren he'd lost track of.

Buddy strode across the stage and gave each a warm hug. "It's so good to see you, Mr. and Mrs. ~~Rodell~~," he said. MCGRAE

They were his folks. But they weren't the old, spent folks he'd shut the coffin lids on back in the 2010s. They were the parents he'd had when he 16 and still living at home. The ones who'd raised him and his brothers to be independent and resented it when he became exactly what they'd intended, just the way he did when any loved one started doing things with minds of their own.

He loved his parents with his whole heart, but the teen years had left scars on the relationship that never fully healed. Ever since he was a teenager who loved reading comic books, Marty had been the kind of guy who would have reveled in being a heroic crime fighter with Super Vision. But he couldn't stand the thought of any ordinary supervision. It rankled him and that's why he'd chosen to earn the majority of his money hustling golf.

"Son!" said his father. "It's so good to see you!"

"My baby!" Mom said. "I was so excited to learn you'd be in one place long enough for us to stop by and that you'd actually agree to be seen in public with us."

Marty looked down at his own hands. They were gnarled with arthritis and age. He still appeared to himself as scarred by the ancient elements as a prairie barn weather vane, but to his parents he appeared as the little mischievous little boy they were always after to clean up his room. It made him awkward the way it used to when Mom would bang on his locked door with suspicions he'd been up to something naughty adolescent boys do behind locked doors.

"Hey! Good to see you guys!" he said. "Gosh, it's been a long time."

He tried to get up and hug them but the giant blue breast chair would not relinquish its hold. His mother seemed to sense it as an affront. She turned to her husband and gave him a tight little smile.

"You haven't seen your mother in 40 years and you can't give her a hug?"

Marty tried again in vain to rise and could not. He shrugged. "No, sorry. Can't," he said without explanation.

They looked at each other and Marty saw a familiar wave of disappointment crest over their faces. No matter how much you love your parents or how much you love your children, the the relationship is designed to fracture, the sole exception being the sparkling love between grandparents and their grandchildren. He'd heard "Roots" author Alex Haley, as expert on family dynamics as any man who'd ever lived, say it was because grandchildren and grandparents are united by their hatred of a common enemy.

Part of that was why Marty was such a distracted parent. He had great relations with all his children as soon as he removed himself from all their lives. Nuclear families, he believed, often failed because of all the inherent radioactivity. On top of all that were the myriad divorces, the bastard children and all the oversexed infidelity that combined to leave so many American family trees all forked up.

But like most children, he truly and rapturously loved his folks. He remembered so many wondrous times with them as a child, to the point where he wondered if that had been the best time of his life and he'd been steadily rolling downhill ever since he was 2. They'd enveloped him and his brothers with true love. He never remembered his father going to work. He didn't know where he got the money to take the family on beach vacations or to Disney World, but he always managed. And he ran effective interference any time Mom tried to soften the boys up.

Once when the four were playing football on a muddy spring day, Mom fretted that they were tearing up the lawn and it would be unsightly throughout the remainder of the season. "We're not raising grass, Rachel, we're raising boys."

Marty figured his life-long resistance to work, his fondness for revelry and strong spirits all came straight from Dad, a party animal who'd checked out with a fatal heart attack in 2004. Marty vividly recalled the time Mom had dragged them all to family enhancement seminar at the local church. He remembered Dad's seething exasperation at the prissy instructor's insistence on teaching teens how to live.

Marty felt an electrifying shiver in his bowels when Dad stormed out and said, "*I'm* going to live and let them watch." He went right to the bar to watch the hockey game. It became an instant and indelible lesson for Marty. He often wished he could have met his father outside the bounds of their genealogical constraints. He was sure they'd have been buds.

Mom always seemed to Marty like a stagecoach driver trying to slow a runaway rig down a narrow mountain pass. She'd had her hands full with Dad, Marty and his brothers Tom and Judas, the youngest whom everyone called Jack. Children ruin women, Marty believed, and his Mom was Exhibit A. He was sure she had to have been a lot of fun to have attracted a man as lively and engaging as Russ McCrae. But trying to raise a family takes a toll no women should want.

He vowed to make it up to her when dementia set it and he was sure the end was near. In the end, "near" had been 46 torturous months. He was more shocked than ashamed the day when the casual thought floated across his mind that he could solve a lot of their mutual problems by just pressing the accelerator and running Mom over.

Thirty seconds previous she'd shot him a vicious look and snarled that he was a cruel and indifferent son. She said he'd tossed out a bag of sacred family treasures into the trash and just couldn't wait for her to die. The bag had been full of expired coupons, old car care tips and ancient e-mail jokes with punchlines involving people like Monica Lewinsky.

It had been trash all right and that meant she'd only been half right.

He'd kept his vow to be the good son, better than even the sainted Judas/Jack. Marty was the one stationed at the apartment where she lived alone since Dad died in 2004. He was the one who took her grocery shopping and to get her hair cut. He was the one who never loses his patience with her.

"Yes, Mom."

"That's right, Mom."

"It'll be okay, Mom."

Two weeks after she no longer has the cognitive power to recognize it, he'd finally become the properly mannered son she'd worked so hard to raise. Seeing his mother turn so bad, so quickly, was like hearing a corrupt judge in a Turkish court sentence him to prison for drug charges of which he was innocent.

During the long nights spent with the woman who no longer recognized him and he no longer loved, he wondered if he'd ever feel guilt about the day he thought, "Man, I could end her suffering and mine by just gunning the accelerator and putting the dear old girl down."

He knew he'd pay for all his iniquities. He already was. Not killing her nearly killing him. He came to conclude that every time he'd make a sarcastic or insincere jab, God would add 18 months to her life.

Later he mused God had added them all to Marty's.

But eventually she did die. Eventually, everyone did.

Life's poignant ache was never far from Mary's heart. Seeing his parents made him wish he could have known them from before he'd ever been born. He knew instinctively they were special.

The only problem was they never stopped seeing him like he was 16-year-old misfit trying to get away with something. In many ways, that's exactly what he'd always been.

"How you feeling these days, son?" Dad asked. "I hope you're not still sneaking beers."

Marty told him that he felt good considering he was pushing 115 years old. "My big complaint is that I used to be able to piss over a boxcar and now it just dribbles down on my feet. Of course, with the fancy doodads on that bed back at the Bolten, I never need to leave the mattress to relieve myself. It's all absorbed, transformed and, I think, run through the coffee filters down in the cafeteria."

"Son, please, watch your potty mouth!"

"Sorry, mom."

"You're not still running around with that Ben Carlisle are you?"

"No, mom. He was killed in an automobile accident in 1998."

"What about that awful Andy Norman?"

"Cancer got him in 2017."

"Well, that's good. That boy was always trouble."

"Who are you taking to the prom this year, son?" Dad said. "I know the way that Becky Kephart looks at you means she'd go. Have you thought about asking her?"

"I won't be going to the prom this year."

They gave each other quick, forlorn glances. It seemed to Marty they were concerned about his sexuality, but maybe he was reading too much into it.

"How are you getting along with your brothers, Marty? You guys not fighting too much, are you?"

"I dreamed about Tommy the other night," Marty said. "We were playing catch and there was a donkey in a sombrero like the one right over there."

"How about Jack? You know he idolizes you," Mom said.

"I miss Judas. Judas was the best. I remember telling him secrets I'd never tell anyone else. You could always trust Judas."

"Well, son, we have to go. Will we be seeing you soon?"

"I sure hope so. Where are you guys living now?"

"We're right where we've always been, son," Dad said. "We're right where we belong. Goodbye."

"Hey before you guys go," Marty said, "I just want to tell you how much I love you guys. You were the best parents a kid could ever have. I'm sorry I didn't treat you better and I hope you can forgive me. I love you guys. I love you with all my heart."

"Thank you son," Mom said, sweetly. "Oh, and one more thing."

"Yes, Mom?

"Please clean your room. We're expecting company tonight."

"Yes, Mom."

SEPTEMBER 2079

Marty was staring at Buster, who was staring at the TV. Staring at Marty was Darlene O'Day, an otherwise mild-mannered receptionist from an accounting firm just blocks from the ornate verging on gaudy front doors of the Bolten. She was one of the most persistent players and enjoyed Gold Card status, which entitled her to gift shop discounts and free sodas at the concession stands. Marty knew a little bit about her — name, occupation, interests — because Buster had employed every conceivable way to wring each and every dime out of the paying public. And that was everyone.

Polls showed that 97.8 percent of those surveyed expressed positive feelings toward *Excesstival!!!* and intended to gamble on McCrae's death. Of those, 68 percent indicated they would play multiple times. Nearly a quarter of them vowed they intended to travel more than five hours to play multiple times. Nine percent of the true fanatics lived within two hours and said they'd play every chance they got.

Then there were the 2 percenters like the 49-year-old O'Day. They would play every spare moment with every spare dime. O'Day was a divorced single mom of two teenage boys. Marty could tell she hated her job dealing daily with accountants and their overwrought customers. She never said much, but Marty could read her all her Caribbean daydreams. For many of the customers, especially ones like her, he felt a poignant chagrin that he couldn't just up and die for them.

He might have willed himself to do so, too, if he could have been assured his soul would get to stick around long enough to watch her go off her rocker. It was destined to be a merry celebration. Truly, he could sense she was trapped by life. He figured she'd spent already nearly $1,200 in visits. He could have ascertained precisely if he'd bothered to check with Buster, but he didn't like engaging Buster in any such tedious talks.

Buster reminded him in many ways of 7 or 8 of his more morose fathers-in-law. He was consumed with money and Marty felt a quick sort of pity for him. It always passed in a flash. He'd learned long ago that there was nothing he could do to help men or women who'd been born or raised to regard the accumulation of money as the sole motivation for daily respiration.

Buster was one of those people Marty felt would have benefitted from a tribal upbringing from the 18th century. Those nomadic folks weren't consumed with acquisition. They were consumed with survival. They'd roam The Great Plains in search of food. They would take what they needed and leave the rest behind. They learned to respect and not overuse the resources with which they were bestowed. But Buster, like so many of his 21st century brethren, was born vapid. Survival was never a question so he became consumed with consumption. It made Marty want to shake some sense into his shell.

It was a pity, Marty felt, that meddling wouldn't help. He wanted to educate the lad. He was miffed that Buster never wanted to talk or ask him questions when men and women from all over the solar system came in every day to seek his wisdoms or make small talk. So he resorted to tough love, one of his favorite emotional responses. Tough love meant Marty could be as cruel and indifferent to anyone as long is it was under the guise of tough love.

He exploited the opportunity any time he'd spy the candle in Buster's pumpkin begin to flicker and that happened every time Dudash entered the room. He'd make awkward conversation and stumbling attempts to appear engaging. It never worked and Buster asked Marty why not.

"Well, Buster, you have two things going against you: you're a moron and she's not. The combination constructs a nearly insurmountable obstacle for some one tends toward density, as do you. She's a refined and smashing young lady who yearns to live life with a gusto unquenched and all you do is sit her, watch TV and count money in your head," Marty said.

Buster chuckled. Marty sensed it was impossible to insult him and thought it might grow tiresome just trying. Yet, there were times when Marty suspected Buster was always in on the joke, that there was a subcutaneous craftiness that, much like Will Ponce, allowed him to set a goal and achieve it, two disciplines that had forever eluded Marty. And in spite of it all, Marty liked him. He had a great capacity for humanity and all its struggles. Plus, with Buster he had no need to harness piercing honesty with tact.

"You look bored whenever any one's talking about anything that isn't you," Marty said. "You exhibit no compassion for the everyday struggles of your fellow man. You're unread, you never smile, you don't make eye contact. If your body is, as the Bible says, a temple, then you've urinated all over the altar. You rarely glance away from the television and the reason people are afraid to get near you is because you look like someone who smells bad."

Buster wheezed out some barks of laughter.

"See, there you go," Marty said. "I just hit you with a nasty string of insults and you chuckle like a rooster with a pine cone caught in his throat.""Well, it's funny to me because I'm right where I need to be," he said. "Thanks to you, it's all going according to plan. I want to make a lot of money before I'm ready to settle down."

Marty recognized it as flawed logic. Throughout his life, anyone he'd ever met who'd been the least bit interested in making money never had the slightest idea of how to enjoy any of it. They'd acquire things for reasons of status, but got only the least base enjoyments of them. They didn't revel in life's gifts. It's like they'd grown up playing competitive Monopoly with life or death stakes.

Again, it was like that with Will Ponce, too. He had genius for making money and probably made more out of it than anyone, but he never knew the first thing about enjoying its benefits. It was astounding to Marty that anyone could spend as much time as Will did with him and not adopt any of his lazy habits. Maybe it was like in a marriage where the spouse takes the opposite trait of the other to give the marriage balance; if one's cheap, the other becomes extravagant.

That was Marty's job, he always felt.

"I've seen it a thousand times, Buster," he said. "You're doing really well right now, yes?"

Buster gave a slow nod. He'd already cleared over $4 million in fees and endorsements alone. He'd be due commissions and cuts when the thing got wrapped up, but that would be up to the lawyers.

"Yet, guaranteed, when I go, you won't take a cruise or go hiking. All you'll do is figure out a way to perpetuate my legacy so you can squeeze every last dime out of my decaying corpse. C'mon, admit it."

It was true. McCrae had already decided to will his body to science and Buster knew he couldn't talk him out of it. But Buster still had hopes he could persuade him into having his remains emulsified so people could rent out him out for things like tailgate parties.

"Life is about experiences, not acquisitions," Marty explained. "Take the fair Dudash just out yonder. She didn't take this job for money. She took it because she thought it would be fun. She's someone who'd be easy to engage at a party. The more you know about her, the more interesting she becomes. With you, it's just the opposite. The more I know about you the less likely I am to dig deeper. You're shallow as a plate of warm piss. You're like a character in one of those old Woody Allen movies. The sad thing is I know I could help you and it frustrates me. We spend all this time together and you rarely inquire about my life and my wisdoms. How about we change that starting today? Let's turn that television off and you start paying attention to what's being said in here. We can make it a project. It'll be fun. What do you say?"

Buster was silent for a moment then he nodded and said, "Well, you've given me a lot to think about. I do have one question."

"Yes?"

"Just one."

"Well?"

"What's an Allen movie and what makes it woodie?"

Marty just shook his head and Buster resumed watching TV. Time expired on Darlene O'Day and she dropped from site, walked through the gift shop, grabbed a free Dr. Pepper at the concession stand, and got right back in line. Tuesdays were slow and she could usually play two or three times over lunch before summoned back to her world of accountants, numbers and daydreams of a better life.

⁓〜⁓

The transparent sleep gauze draped over McCrae's bed began to rise as if by magic. It was 4:30 a.m., a time when players would drift in and silently pray for the death of the sleeping McCrae, who was usually sound asleep from 1 a.m. till 5 a.m. The sleep gauze was invented in 2023 by an insomniac Alabamian who'd been robbed of his rest by the neighbor's yapping hound dogs. It effectively screened out the sounds of barking dogs, passing sirens, partying neighbors and other nightly annoyances that made modern living so difficult on light sleepers. It would have made Lance Cunningham a fortune, too, had he not died tragically at the age of 47, just one year after he invented the Bark Blanket. The device was also effective at screening out well-meaning neighbors the night they dashed into his smoke-filled doorway to helpfully shriek, "Run for your life! Your house is on fire!"

Dingus, who'd set the trapdoor on "automatic," was snoring loudly in the garishly upholstered recliner that had become his bedroom. He had strict orders not to disturb McCrae's sleep until 6 a.m., or in the event of fire. Cunningham's untimely demise had not been in vain.

But now the gauze soundlessly rose and McCrae awoke.

Before him stood a shimmering vision of a mythic man. His golden, curly hair fell to shoulders so well-rounded it looked as if he were smuggling coconuts in his double breasted mohair jacket. Pleated white ruffles billowed up to his neck like frothy waves racing up a beach. Flawlessly tailored white pants clung to his sculpted buttocks and seemed to ripple down his long, athletic legs rooted in rattlesnake cowboy boots.

McCrae's rubbed the sleep from his eyes and stared in disbelief. It was dy Ego, the old alien impostor.

"Hello, Martin," he said. His supermodel smile was lighthouse bright. Marty had spent nearly two years with dy Ego on the planet Gonto and the extraterrestrial had become one of his most dear friends. He cherished him so much that he was nearly able to conceal his disappointment — his greatest disappointment — that upon his arrival he was told he'd missed Jesus by just two days. What he didn't know, either, was that had he stayed just two days longer, he would have been there for Jesus's return. Jesus loved corn and Gontoians grew really great corn.

"dy Ego!" McCrae gushed, his smile its own warming beacon. "Am I dreaming?"

"Certainly not! We'd heard about this foolishness and I was chosen to come and find out what you're up to. But tell me: how on Earth did you recognize me?"

McCrae's grin widened. "I'd recognize you anywhere, I don't care how elaborate your disguise. But, I must say, you look magnificent. You look like you walked off the cover of a romance novel. Did you come to Earth to experience carnal pleasures?"

dy Ego threw his head back and laughed. In the corner, Buster stirred. "No, my motives are pure. A visit with you will be plenty pleasurable. We're here for just a day or so."

"Just a day or so? Can't you stay longer?"

dy Ego laughed, then tapped a long, gold-ringed finger under his chin. "Yes, you know we love to visit, but we never stay long. As you have said many times, Earth is populated by too many, um, what do you call them? Burning orifices?"

"Flaming assholes."

"Yes, too many flaming assholes. If your planet had better mannered people it would be overrun with galactic tourists."

In the corner, Buster snorted a bit as his uneven sleep cycle hit a speed bump. His lips made light motorboat sounds as the back of his right hand ran up under his nose while his left hand clawed at his crotch. dy Ego saw this distasteful display and immediately deduced Buster was a burning orifice.

"But what are you going to do if I croak in the next —" he glanced up at the digital clock — "12 minutes and 38 seconds. You'll have all that money. What are you going to do?"

"Ha! You know how little we care for money, Martin," he said. "Remember, we are a very contented people. And you, my friend, you won't be dying any time soon."

Marty leaned forward on his elbows. "You know something I don't?"

"Well, when we heard you were involved with this nonsense, we retrieved your mortality scans produced after the chip we put in your butt began functioning."

Marty reflexively sparked with anger. "Geez, what is it with you bastards and all these butt chips? That's very inconsiderate!"

Marty was always sore when the subject of alien butt chips came up. He'd repeatedly scolded them on their intrusive use of the devices. They'd always deny using them, but when push came to shove . . .

"What can I say? Old habits die hard. Anyway we can't predict when you're going to die, of course, but our tests indicate it ought not to be for a while. Your heart alone could beat until you're 130 years old. You're living in a perfectly controlled environment. They see to your every need. Stresses are low. You're more likely to die of boredom than natural causes."

The thought hadn't occurred to Marty. He, like everyone else, assumed he was going to expire rather shortly. That was fine with him. The thought that he could be endlessly cooped up in this glorified intensive care unit as a parade of greedy strangers came by to pray for his death had never dawned on him.

"Any chance those tests of yours could be wrong?"

"No chance," dy Ego said. "You're remarkably healthy for your advanced Earth years. And, remember, these were our modern tests, the ones we implemented after your recommendations."

"Ah, yes. The post-rectal probe years," he chuckled. "Whose bright idea was it to learn all there is to learn about humans by examining them through the bodily portal from which they deposited all their foul-smelling wastes?"

"The arguments on behalf of the method were sound," he said with the detachment of a proctological scholar. "But it was all for naught. A lot of good equipment and research was wasted on that particular procedure. We really thought we were doing the right thing. All the humans we'd examined, as soon as we brought them into the white room, boy, the first thing they'd do was drop their pants and bend over. Then you told us all the Earthlings thought that's the way aliens examined them. They were just being cooperative. It's a good thing you spoke up or aliens around the galaxy would still be shoving those confounded probes up the rectums of poor, bent-over Earthlings."

"No, as I told you before, most of us can't stand to have anything shoved up our butts. Hurts like hell. Open up and say, 'Ow!'"

They both laughed as the clock ticked away. Buster, who was unaccustomed to any night noises, was growing more restless with the happy chatter.

"So tell me, we all want to know," dy Ego said. "Why did you get involved in this nonsense?"

McCrae settled back against the inclined bed, his hands behind his head, knees scrunched up under the covers. He cocked his head to the right and said, "I dunno. I was terribly bored. All my friends, every one of them, were dead. Even the last of the five Rexes, including the Nervous Rex, had died. The last 20 years had been terribly lonely. My life was full and I was ready to die, but at the end of your life when you know your days on Earth are literally numbered, time stands still. Buster over there came up with a plan so I would no longer be bored."

dy Ego's face saddened, making it even more beautiful. "I wish we'd have known. We could have brought you back to Gonto. You could have spent your remaining days with us. You'd have for sure met Jesus by now. He's been back many, many times. The guy just can't get enough of our corn."

"I thought about it. Some of my happiest days were spent with you and your people on your lovely little planet, and I'm still dying to meet Jesus. But I really love the people here. They work hard and they play hard. They're tough, blunt, rude, insensitive and they laugh too loud. They fight hard in the face of adversity and struggle to make meaningless lives fulfilling. I have a great respect for the persevering human spirit. I love being human and I love human beings."

The clock registered just 30 seconds as dy Ego stood astride the black X. Marty asked if he'd see him again.

"You may, but you may not recognize me. I'm a master of disguise, you know," he said with a wink.

"You are a master of self-delusion. Say, if you have time, stop by central Indiana. I swear, it's the place on Earth that looks most like Gonto. Just miles and miles of corn spiking up out of the ground. It looks just like somebody came over and gave the whole planet a giant crew cut."

… 14 … 13 … 12 …

"I will try, Martin."

… 11 … 10 … 9 …

"And tell my friends on Gonto how very much I miss them."

… 8 … 7 … 6 …

"I will. And Martin?"

"Yes, dy Ego?"

… 5 … 4 … 3 …

"Remember: Humiliation, poverty, hopelessness, — you've already survived far worse than death."

… 2 … 1 …

ding!

The trapdoor opened. The Coca-Cola jingle was played, but dy Ego, now bathed in a phosphorous glow, seemed to Martin to levitate above the void.

"That which does not kill you …"

"Yes?" Marty said hopefully.

"…can still hurt like hell."

Smiling, he began to slowly drift down into the blackness.

"Well, what's that supposed to mean?"

"All shall be explained. Goodbye, my friend!" he called out. Then — *wheeeeeee!!!!!* — he was gone. The door closed and another contestant, this one an elderly church choir director with rosary beads in her hands and evil greed in her eyes, stood there baffled by the way time'd seemed to stall.

Buster had been awaked by the brightening glow off the peculiar, beautiful man from Gonto. He rubbed his eyes hard, blinked twice and pushed the buzzer that signaled Nurse Dudash, who was working a rare nightshift at the desk just outside the suite.

"Yes?"

"Dudash, have the food from Booker's Deli retested for hallucinogens. And have a bottle of Wild Turkey sent up. I'm having trouble sleeping again."

MARCH 2080

The world was practically throbbing with earnest young men and women in the latter part of the 21st century. Many of them floated into sessions with McCrae in hopes he could provide enlightenment in nimble little increments. Their visits provoked from him the most elaborate lies.

Benjamin Sellers had the squarish features that made him look to Marty like he'd been constructed entirely out of Legos. Marty supposed a block-head like Sellers would be smarter than kiddie toys, but two weeks of steady visits was proving otherwise. He was one of Marty's favorite contestants because Sellers took him his every word at face value and transcribed it all into the thesis he was preparing about the past and future of sex. It was certainly Marty's favorite topic. And as long as Marty humbled himself with some manufactured missteps, Sellers would buy anything, even though he kept telling him to verify his wildest assertions. But Sellers, who'd made more than 20 visits over a two-week period, could not be dissuaded. He was well-scrubbed, cheerful and open and honest as a Midwestern mini-mart where they left out the honor box when the clerk needed to use the toilet. There was always something about those qualities that Marty felt obliged to corrupt.

"I guess by now my biggest miscalculation was my long-held belief that Jesus was going to return during my lifetime and informed stunned believers that the Ten Commandments contained a typo," Marty said. "I've read Biblical scholars who believe the Seventh Commandment has been misinterpreted. It should read, they say, 'Thou shalt commit adultery.' Really, I'm surprised He hasn't been back yet to straighten things out here. Of course, we didn't treat Him so well last time He was here, did we?"

"No, sir, we did not!" Sellers said, shaking his head. "Pray tell, what are some of the prognostications of which you're most proud."

Marty had been painting the magnificent cityscape at the easel near the balcony window and put down the brush to give Sellers his full attention. "I foresaw by about 10 years the trend that women would begin having unusual breast implants scattered around their bodies to seize the interests of the breast obsessed."

He told Sellers about the woman in 2018 who had two big breasts implants installed beneath her shoulder blades because her boyfriend refused to slow dance with her. The breast implants turned him into an avid dancer. And he said he wasn't surprised when breast escalation led to some women to eschew two big breast implants in favor of one big one where the cleavage used to be.

Just picking up steam, Marty continued, "The brassiere industry was, of course, predictably supportive. I rather enjoyed those mono-breasts, myself. I'd always felt like one breast was getting jealous or lonely if I was devoting all my attention to the other. My friends said I was crazy for feeling that way, but I've always been more sensitive than my friends."

Marty said he was pleased in 2021 to have finally persuaded pointy-headed engineers at NASA to cease studying the mating habits of insects, frogs and worms and finally give the people what they wanted: a chance to study the mating habits of orbiting astronauts. The resulting pay-per-view was so successful, he said, that NASA went private and space sex subsequently took off like a rocket.

"I was there at lift off and was the second recreation director for the first lunar resort," he said. "They sent for me when all those suicidal lunar nudists exploded after defying warnings that a Skins vs. Skins volleyball match would be fatal in space. It was a terrible scandal and I was called in to clean up the mess. Well, the PR mess. As we found out in those early days, there's no real mess to speak of when a human body boils in its own blood."

Sellers was eager to learn about Charlie "Moon Beam" McCoy, the first child conceived and raised in outer space. Did McCrae know him?

"Know him? I was the kid's godfather," he said. "His dad and I were golfing buddies and his mom used to wait on tables at the Lunar-Tics Saloon. I introduced them. Eight months later when they were married, I was the best man. The doctors were worried he'd be some kind of freak and got his folks all worried. Well, I knew he was going to be some kind of freak, but not the kind that should worry anyone. They trusted me to represent him in negotiations with NBA teams before he was old enough to drive his first lunar rover. And you know how that all ended."

"Boy, do I," Sellers gushed. "I was at the arena when he scored 158 points to lead the those perennial doormats, the L.A. Clippers, to their first of six consecutive championships. All thanks to the 8-foot-4 Moon Beam McCoy. These days, you can't even think of playing in the NBA unless you've spent your formative years shooting moon hoops."

They talked about the tumult from 2025 when terrorists botched an attempt to topple the Washington Monument, named in honor of one of America's beloved Founding Fathers. They'd only succeeded in knobbing off the point at the top.

"By then the nation's capital had finally begun to get perspective along with a sense of humor," McCrae said. "Remember, that was the year late night TV comics prevailed on the United Nations to send all our most incorrigible prisoners from throughout the solar system to a penal colony on Uranus. It was about at the same time when I was golfing with, coincidentally enough, President Bolten. He was wondering how he should address the restoration of the landmark when I convinced him that we should save money, leave it like it was, and rename it the Clinton Monument in honor of President Bill Clinton, one of our nation's Fondling Fathers."

It was the same pivotal year, McCrae said, that the brassiere industry reported a milestone that, thanks to moon and planetary colonization, it was for the first time manufacturing more undergarments designed to hold breasts down rather than lift them up.

"Really, this is all fascinating," Sellers said. "But what about the future? What can you tell me about the future of sex? That's what interests me."

Over in the corner, Buster momentarily glanced away from the television to hear McCrae's response. He knew it was going to be a string of whoppers and that was the only thing that could get Buster to divert his attention from "The Price is Right."

Asked to play the mystic, McCrae was flawless. He adopted a faraway gaze and prophesied, "I will share all I know. I believe I can see the end of humanity. It is not far off and all our wounds are self-inflicted."

"In the year 2098, super-intelligent extraterrestrials will invade the Earth with the warlike intent of enslaving our women," he said with gravity. "They abruptly and peacefully depart when our wise leaders tell them the only way to do so is to locate what was once faddishly known as their G spots."

As time was ticking down on Sellers, McCrae picked up the pace and began to forecast with an increasing dread about how in 2110, after years of costly failure, manufacturers would perfect a virtual reality sex machine ready for distribution to the eager masses. It would allow users to have any kind of sex with anyone they want at anytime they want and for as often and as long as they want.

"It will be safe, efficient and fun," McCrae said. "But in 2165 after nearly four decades of decreasing human interaction, the last of the human race will expire never realizing that virtual reality sex, while an entertaining pastime, does nothing to perpetuate the species."

As Sellers's time ticked down to seconds, McCrae cheerfully closed with, "And then in the year 2199, super-intelligent cockroaches will speculate human beings died out from too much sex. The controversial so-called 'Big

Bang' theory will be greeted by other roaches with scholarly bemusement. And that's how I foresee the future."

"Thank you, Mr. McCrae!" Sellers said. "You have no idea how helpful and entertaining you — *wheeee … eeeeee …!!!*"

Marty smiled, pleased with himself at how well he timed the end of human existence to coincide with that of the wide-eyed Sellers. He turned to Buster as another contestant rolled to the top of the X in a seamless second. "Well, not bad, if I do say so myself."

Buster gave an appreciative nod with his face creasing into a faint smile, "That one was pretty good, boss. Pretty good, indeed."

It pleased Marty to see that Buster had begun paying attention, if only just a bit.

❦

Marty was endlessly fascinated by how others earned their daily bread. He'd ask shoe salesmen their feelings about feet. He asked chefs at fancy restaurants if they ever chowed on stuff from the local crap shack. He asked a cookie maker from a Berlin, Pennsylvania, factory if any elf-like people worked on the line with him. And he so relentlessly probed a poor proctologist from Poughkeepsie that the man who thought he'd heard it all began wondering if friends really did refer to him behind his back as the Rear Admiral.

And he was overjoyed when thin and pretty Grace Nelson answered his question about her occupation by saying, "I'm a Vanderbilt University history professor focusing on the study of the Middle Ages."

"Whose Middle Ages?"

"Why, mankind's, of course," she said with a trace of scholarly exasperation. "The Middle Ages are the Earthly epoch from roughly 500 BC to 1600 BC. Certainly a man as learned as yourself knows that much."

Marty tried to appear sage by nodding and saying, "Yes, of course, but what you're really telling me is that you're a gypsy, a teller of fortunes."

She smiled, wrinkled an eyebrow and asked what he meant.

"I mean that anyone who claims to profess they know the time of the planet's Middle Ages by very definition must know when the world will end. You can't define the middle of something unless you are certain of its end."

She shook her head in a slow, teasing scold. "I'm unprepared to have to defend a long accepted field of study."

"Is that so?" Marty asked. "Well, how old are you?

"I'm 46."

"Ah, then you are considered a middle aged woman, correct?"

"Yes, the commonly accepted actuarial tables would indicate I'm at the midway point in my life."

It was times like this when Buster inadvertently felt himself pointing the remote at the humans in the room instead of the television wishing he could change the channel. Even in mere 15-minute increments, these McCrae logistics drove him nuts.

But Marty was on a roll. He said as of that day he wasn't middle aged until he'd reached 57 — and that would only count if he dropped dead in the next day or so. No one knew how long he was going to live.

"And, really, who says I'm not middle aged right now? Heck, we could be on the verge of some life-prolonging breakthrough that would mean I'm really only reaching some sort of puberty right now. We just don't know, but calling me, anyone or any human epoch 'middle aged' seems like a god-like prognostication. When I look back on my Earth life, I've always felt sort of Martian. When I was your age, 46, I remember I felt like I felt when I was about 24.3 or the same age as if I'd spent my entire life circling the sun on the planet Mars. I felt like I was born 12. But soon after that age I started sneaking beers and felt immediately about 16. Then I endured all the adolescent hallmarks of a 16 year old — no money, awkward around the girls, lived with my parents — until I was about 24. And I felt about 24 until I was 46."

He told how when he was 24 he'd worked one poverty-stricken summer as a newspaper writer in Nelson's Nashville hometown. For the purposes of their discussion about Mars and Earth years, he told her she could refer to the now-defunct paper as "The Daily Planet."

"Hungover or not, it was my duty to be at my desk at every morning by 6 a.m.," he said. "During those pitiless pre-dawn mornings when roosters were still snoozing, it was often my job to write about the daily doom befalling numerous central Tennessee men and women. I often wrote about people who were expiring in what people called their middle ages. Their obituaries revealed their middle ages had been two decades previous. I remember thinking, 'Well, it's a shame that drunken farmer stumbled into that rusty combine. But, hey, the guy was 46. He lived a good full life.' At 24, I thought 46 was a long life."

It had really colored his perceptions, he said. He'd spent a good deal of his life thinking about death. Ever since he'd turned about 90, he'd just been hoping he could get on with it.

"See, I have no fear of death as long as it doesn't have to hurt," he said. "I began praying that my accidentally death would come after I'd skipped off a sidewalk directly in front of a speeding bus I'd never see coming. I began hoping some 24-year-old Earth reporter would arrive at the scene and get quotes from startled eye witnesses who'd swear they saw my soul shoot straight to heaven. And that my soul wasn't wearing any pants."

As her time ticked down, Marty apologized for having dominated the conversation. Still, he reiterated his belief that only scarf draped fortune tellers could call anyone middle aged.

"And, Grace, I hope your true middle ages, no matter how old you are today, remain many happy Martian years from now."

She thanked him and without ever realizing it at the time became an instant convert to his thinking, dashing nearly two decades of intensive study on what she would no longer call the Middle Ages. Within weeks, she poured her heart into a beautifully written and thoughtful treatise arguing that it was time to rename The Middle Ages something more optimistic concerning the planet's longevity. The paper was roundly ridiculed. She lost her job and spent the rest of her once-promising career writing obituaries for the on-line Nashville news gatherers. She thought of McCrae anytime some drunken 46-year-old Tennessee farmer stumbled into a rusty combine and their survivors said it was such a sad, sad shame for someone to be cut down in their middle ages.

⸺✸⸺

Rounds of golf were never far from Marty's mind. Golf provided him with a spiritual solace unmatched elsewhere in his life. Even during competitive matches with tens of thousands of dollars at stake, he often thought more about God when he golfed than when he was seated in worshipful church pews, were he was usually consumed with thoughts of screwing the church organist.

One of his first few wives, Becky, was a Lutheran church organist. He loved her deeply and his mind often wandered straight to sex whenever the preacher was in the pulpit blahbidy-blahbidy-blahhing about the eternal salvation of his miserable soul.

It was different on golf courses. At peace with man and nature, he believed there'd be golf in heaven and he couldn't wait to see the courses. He was hoping to ask Jesus all about it. He remained on a life-long quest to meet Jesus, and not just in a spiritual way. It infuriated him that all his life he'd been told that Jesus saw everything all the time. If that was so, why was He such a idle bystander to so much human misery? Marty wanted to interrogate the ever-elusive Lord.

For nearly the entirety of his life, Marty remained the best golfer no one had ever heard of it, and that was fine with him. He was a professional golf hustler, one of the best. He'd work the world and would always pack his clubs whenever Will invited him to accompany him on business trips to luxurious resorts plush, pluckable pigeons. And the one time each year Will knew that Marty would be absent was during the last three weeks of March when he'd jet down to Florida's Space Coast for golf and blessed spring baseball. That's when the yearly gathering of fat defense contractors, retired military brass and NASA engineers met for their annual bacchanal. These were men and women who wrongly concluded they could construct a solid golf game based on the coincidental fact they'd help put a men on the moon, Mars and various other once desolate and forlorn sites around the universe. Golf should be easy, they figured. After all, they were a bunch of rocket scientists.

The hours from 3 a.m. to 6 a.m. were the most quiet at the Bolten. The drunks had come and gone and the coffee-chugging Type A's had yet to charge in for a quick chance on McCrae. The men and women who drifted in during those wee hours were sleepwalkers or dead on their feet. Conversation was nearly non-existent. McCrae rarely slept for more than an hour at a time throughout the day. Even when he was awake in the early morning hours, he usually just sat there quietly in bed and thought of Brick Ryder and the nearly two years Ryder'd stolen from him. He supposed he thought about him with the same level of malevolence that Palley reserved for him and Will.

He thought about what he'd missed on earth, the death of Buddy, what he'd gained on the planet Gonto and how close he'd come to meeting Jesus.

Ryder was a razor-ribbed and gun-faced orbital engineer with the ill-tempered disposition of a mink at the gates of the fur factory. Back in 2022, Marty had managed to clean Ryder out of more than $12,000 in golf wagers. And then, as during the next six years, Ryder swore his bitter oath at him and made Marty come back for rematches that wound up costing Ryder an ever-escalating sum that eventually totaled $550,000. Ryder was very competitive, hated losing, and hated losing to someone he deemed as inferior as Marty. No one had lost more to Marty, and Marty generally shunned repeat pigeons. Too dangerous to risk such hostility. But Ryder was a jerk, loaded with illicit tax dollars, arrogance and had a mean streak that made humility lessons fun to inflict.

Marty always thought about Ryder during the early spring. That was when he'd always conclude his tour of Florida golf resorts with a lucrative visit to the Space Coast and a satisfying spanking of one of NASA's finest, in fact, the guy who planned the routes of the intergalactic space transports.. He was young, bright, had a great future with the space program and Marty was looking forward to a long life of being enriched by Brick Ryder.

He'd never told anyone about his twenty-three months on the distant planet. No one ever learned of Ryder's treacherous revenge and Marty never did meet Jesus, although, ever the optimist, he was hoping it still might happen in spite of the ever dwindling odds.

MAY 2080

The McCrae exhibits on the museum's 8th floor made no mention of the Poncey Scheme, which wasn't really a scheme at all. It was more like a bouquet of dozens of minor crimes all mashed together in a felonious gumbo so exquisite no cold case forensic chef could discern all the ingredients. Sure, there were detectable dashes of grand theft, pinches of porno, tablespoons of wiretapping, a heaping helping of theft and enough narcotics to give the stew a strong felonious broth. There was some scheming involved and plenty of Ponce, but it wasn't like the more famous Ponzi Scheme which earned millions making suckers out of millions.

The so-called Poncey Scheme earned eventual billions making a sucker out of just one: Marshall Palley Sr. None of the fortune that Ponce was destined to accrue would have come to fruition without the 1992 arrest and the runaway ambitions that waddled along in its wake.

Palley the First hadn't been the first. Neither had Erastus Palley Sr., a poor farmer who'd never caught a break. Erastus the second was, in terms of family history, the first that mattered and the one all the rest revered. He'd made a fortune manufacturing farm machinery that tilled and harvested the rich Ohio earth. The family trajectory indicated that the son, Erastus III, would be the first Palley to attend college, which he did at Kenyon. He was also liberated enough to unshackle the family free of the horrid name Erastus, naming his first born the more Presbyterian-sounding Marshall. And he was the scion groomed for greatness, a calling he assumed with relish.

He'd planned to use his bust of the Ponce-fronted marijuana meadows as a springboard in a law and order campaign to run for Congress. Will had come from a long line of family failures, had been sentenced to 10 years in federal prison, but was able to have the sentence reduced on the grounds after Palley vouched for him with the understanding that Will would reciprocate during an eventual congressional campaign. And that much was all true. While Marty'd spent his time reading Louis L'Amour during his incarceration, Will earned a pharmacological engineering degree and had begun leading prison church services. He counseled drug addicted fellow inmates and took ample notes on which drugs they liked best and why.

His journey through the legal system convinced him that the surest way to get rich was to take something illegal that everyone loved and couldn't live without and provide them with a perfectly legal alternative.

It was strictly business.

When someone wondered to Marty if the incarceration meant Will was in trouble, Marty chuckled and observed, "The only time a guy like Will'll ever encounter a monkey wrench is when he comes across a really loose monkey. Trust me, everything always going to work out for Will."

And that's just what began to happen.

For Will, it was a toss up between engaging in more narcotics, immersing himself in retail pornography or starting up a new religion. He chose mind-altering drugs because of his experience in the field. Maybe one day he'd get around to religion and pornography with an eye on combining the potent trio for maximum profiteering.

His unwitting ally was Palley.

The district attorney wound up co-opting Ponce into his early campaigns as the perfect blend of justice and redemption. He'd bring him on stage and have him tell the story about how he, everyone's Palley, had nabbed him, tossed the book at him and then extended the hand of mercy to the former recidivist who was turning over a new leaf, one that wasn't dried and smoked to achieve a euphoric state.

But by the time Palley was comfortably ahead in the polls and basking in the campaign fawning, a trap had already been set. Suspicious from a stream of credible tips, police ordered a search warrant for Palley's offices where they found stashes of incriminating drugs, pornography and fraudulent phone records to doom the candidate among the conservatives he'd courted. The charges weren't filed until after the election, but the public was outraged by the lurid details. Palley, to his dying day, denied the whole thing and said he'd been set up. He'd squandered most of a family fortune on trying to clear his name and lost the rest trying to win back what he'd already lost.

There was widespread suspicion that Marty'd had something to do with it, something Marty denied as laughable. The caper was much too involved for a renown idler like him, he said. He cared so little about the politics of it that he never even bothered to ask Will if he was behind it or not. But he suspected he was. So did everybody else. People'd ask Marty if he thought if Will had put Buddy up to it. "Not a chance," Marty said. "Police said a large receptacle of pop tabs destined for sick kids and kidney dialysis machines had been carelessly knocked to the floor. Buddy would never have left such a philanthropic treasure behind."

But Buddy knew Will'd met people in prison he could have used like garage tools whenever he needed them. The marijuana farm had been a cash business and no one knew how many rubber banded bundles in old Mason jars had been buried up in those Ohio hills. And Marty knew that right after the scandal, Will began supporting a more liberal candidate who went to Washington where among his first acts was to grant Ponce a patent for an over-the-counter sleep drug that left users in a euphoric state. The drug's only side effect was that it turned the user's urine a deep shade of royal purple.

It wouldn't be long that, thanks to Will, all America was peeing purple.

Marshal Marshall Palley III was thinking about all this as he wandered around the museum and its Acme Pharmaceuticals-sponsored exhibits. The scandal'd stained the Palley family for three generations raised on tales of dashed ambitions, lost fortunes and blame darts aimed squarely at Ponce and Marty.

Now, there was another fortune at stake. And Palley III was determined that it become his. He, too, knew a thing about pharmaceuticals. His frequent visits to see McCrae weren't trips down memory lane. With each visit, he left behind traces of toxins too small to be detected, yet powerful enough over time to kill a frail being. By his calculations, refined and retested near nightly, it would take more than 250 times.

Today would mark his 123rd time. That was 123 times of waiting in line, 123 times of smuggling the contaminant, and 123 times of having to stare as the silent McCrae stared back and the bile of bitter history built up in his throat.

It would all be worth it. He just needed to maintain his determination. It would be the perfect crime. And it would be jackpot justice on an historic scale.

JULY 2080

The sign above the final door beyond the security corridor, past all the gaudy kitsch of the Bolten, had drawn the attention of every single eyeball that had strolled through the front gate. Each contestant stood alone in the isolation chamber for 90 seconds where they were alone with their dreams. For 90 seconds they could do nothing but stare at a gray, tombstone-shaped LED screen that read:

Martin J. McCrae
Dec. 9, 1964 — ????
If he dies, you win …
$252,088,175
… good luck!

And the ticker rolled on.

Dudash sat at the faux nurse's station across the hall from the McCrae's suite. She dressed like a nurse, she acted like a nurse, and people assumed she was a nurse. But her meticulously composed charts contained no vital information concerning the health and care of her lone patient. Instead, they contained phone numbers for delis, pizza & sub shops, Chinese restaurants and gyro joints enriched mostly by Buster. A separate chart, written in code, looked most like a medical document, but had the least to do with anything in the operation of the McCrae death watch. It contained the numbers of nail salons, boutiques and psychic hot lines. It belonged to Dudash. She always packed her own figure-conscious lunch or dinner. The only full-time staffer without a chart was the patient. In the four months since she'd been introduced to him, not once did McCrae make a special request for a meal.

Buster would order whatever he pleased, and McCrae would eat right along with him. Strange, thought Dudash. She figured Buster, who'd already gained about 25 pounds, might die diet before McCrae. Then she learned whatever Buster consumed, McCrae would, too. Same portions, too. Greasy burgers, po' boys, burritos, pepperoni pizzas and donuts for dinner. That was a typical day. She later learned that McCrae's diet had been for the most part a doctor's nightmare since New Year's Day 2068 when he'd recklessly resolved to ignore as too impractical all advice issued by doctors.

His life had been full of spontaneous quests and resolutions, the latest being to coin a word that would earn its way into the most venerable Oxford English Dictionary. As goals went he knew it wasn't like leading his team to a Super Bowl victory, brokering a tricky peace deal between historic hostiles or curing something itchy. It's not even like writing a 75,000-word bestseller, something even marginally literate athletes, drug-abusing rock degenerates and self-degrading reality TV stars have achieved, so how big a deal was that?

He knew any word in any dictionary would endure longer than all but the most classic books by the likes of Shakespeare, Twain and Dickens. If he could land a word in a dictionary, any dictionary, he knew it would endure with barnacle-like tenacity through the ages. Once one gains acceptance, dislodging dictionary words becomes as impossible as removing dogged and ill-conceived traffic lights: no one ever thinks of removing them no matter how little traffic they actually stop.

This somewhat inauspicious goal exacted a tedious toll on contestants who became unwitting targets for his scattergun attempts.

He told a podiatrist from Des Moines that he ought to call the common condition of parasthesia, when a foot falls asleep, "comatoes." "See, it makes more sense," he said. "It's easier for people to comprehend, it doesn't have that loathsome whiff of Latin and, gee, it's just fun to say. Go ahead, Doc, try. Let me hear you say, 'Comatoes!'"

"Comatoes!" the doctor cheerfully obliged. "You're right. Comatoes! It is more fun to say!" McCrae made the doctor promise he'd do his best to spread the word on the word and for a while many people in Des Moines began to complain about suffering from comatoes after sitting in a cramped position in his waiting room for too long.

He didn't have as much success with "glibberish: pointless party chatter between two people who'd rather be talking to anyone else." But that's because he used it in such a pejorative way that subjects usually vacated the room with hurt feelings. An elderly woman from Belgium was asking him questions about his travels to her homeland when he gratuitously insinuated the word into the conversation.

"Well, if you want to hear about that, I suppose it won't be long before this whole discussion devolves into glibberish, don't you think?"

"Beg your pardon?"

"You know, glibberish, the pointless party chatter between two people who'd rather be talking to anyone else. Please don't take offense, but glibberish is the clear result of any such discussion that clearly busts small talk down *to* something the size of insect snacks."

It was offensive so it was bound to offend all but the imbeciles. Of course she took offense. As did others he accused of engaging in glibberish. It was rude and he knew it. He was raised to be polite so he dropped glibberish when anenormously pregnant woman from Kelowna, British Columbia, came by rubbing her belly. He congratulated her then cunningly began dropping series of words he'd long hoped would make their way into the public domain.

"Boy or girl?"

"Yes, one of each. We're having twins!"

"Oh, my, you're certainly in for some strong birthquakes."

"Birthquakes?"

"My, yes. Birthquakes are what doctors have begun calling what are commonly known as labor pains. It was a suggestion I made several years ago to a prestigious panel of OB/GYNs in Montreal," he lied. "They agreed that birthquakes is a more monumental way of saying what had been referred to with the rather pedestrian term, labor pains. Really, labor pains are what factory owners experience when they offer the union reps cheap contracts. So, please be sure to tell your doctor that he'd better start calling them birth quakes or else he'll appear a bit out of touch to his patients."

She seemed pleased to have gained this insider knowledge and promised to share it with her doctor.

"Very good, and I hope your birthquakes are mild and that you avoid going," and he delivered this phrase with dramatic pauses intended to startle the young mother-to-be, *"Stork … Raving … Mad!"*

"Stork … Raving … Mad? What's that?"

Her reaction pleased him. She seemed genuinely frightened that she somehow could become *Stork … Raving … Mad!*

"Stork … Raving … Mad! is becoming the accepted medical term for postpartum depression. Wise doctors have begun using *Stork … Raving … Mad!* instead of postpartum depression because it more aptly conveys the seriousness of what happens to mothers whose post-birth hormones go berserk. But I'm sure it won't happen to you."

She thanked him and promised she'd spread the word back throughout the lovely Okanagan Valley where she lived. He was so pleased with the impression he made on her he spent the next day straining to work both "birthquakes" and *"Stork … Raving … Mad!"* into conversations with men and women who'd never before thought of the gynecological or physiological implications before.

He began a promising string of renaming professions and lifestyles. He dubbed a dapper tailor a "sizemologist." He advised a skilled mechanic to elevate his occupational station by announcing to one and all that henceforth he'd like to be called a "motorvator." He also, thanks to Marty, began telling everyone his cargo pants should be called "CarGo" pants.

Whenever young girls came in looking like they'd starved themselves to appear more like popular Hollywood anorexics, he denounced them as "slimitators." He warned contestants to avoid people who tried to conceal ugly natures with makeup or plastic surgery because they were "shamorous."

He railed against flavorless tree-borne fruit for being what he called "crapples," and he was sympathetic to people who'd been punished by late flights, lost luggage or other travel nuisances frequently associated with "error-planes."

When one pimple-faced young man from Detroit confided he was awkward around the ladies, he took the opportunity to foist the word "teastosterone" on the youth.

"Yes, teastosterone," he said. "It's the surplus hormones that get men so consumed with ambitious lust that women find them universally repulsive. You likely experience a surge of teastosterone whenever you read pornography. The teastosterone overcomes your ability to think rationally, and all you can think about is raw sex. Women sense this and rare is the one who doesn't want to bolt from your presence."

The lad impressed Marty with his first question: "How can I identify that rare woman?"

"You won't. In my time, the only instances where my romantic ardor perfectly equaled a willing woman's was way back in 2015. I was consumed with animal lust for her and she reciprocated with enthusiasm. She refused not a one of my offers. It was a night of unrivaled passion that left us both more satisfied than any encounters previous or since. It was the best $2,500 I'd ever spent."

"She was a prostitute?"

"Yes, but I like to think that was just a coincidence."

As the holidays were nearing, he confided to parents of young children his pretend memory that he suffered from a condition he'd dubbed, "Santaclaustrophobia." "I'd have a fit whenever my mother or father dropped me on the lap of anyone wearing a Santa costume. It frightened the living daylights out of me. I was in therapy over it for years. In fact, many existing fears that bedevil adults are the result of latent Santaclaustrophobia. It's something to watch out for around the holidays. Santaclaustrophobia is harmful to many children."

He thought he'd struck gold when one day in walked a man named James Ewing who said he was a newspaper reporter for a prominent Baltimore newspaper and was there to write a story about McCrae that would be syndicated around the world.

"Eureka!" McCrae said. "You can use the power of the press to help me get a word in the dictionary."

"I'll do my best, but my editor's a tough SOB," Ewing said. "If he senses any crap in a story he cuts it right out. He's the kind of guy who's such a stickler for punctuation that he spends more time inserting unnecessary commas than he does appreciating the style and sense of a well-written story. He's very liberal in his use of punctuation."

In rapid fire, McCrae told him the definitions to the words comatoes, glibberish, birthquakes, motorvator, sizemology, vagatarian, slimitator, shamorous, error-plane, santaclaustrophobia, teastosterone and *Stork … Raving … Mad*!

Ewing recorded the exchange with evident delight. That's why McCrae was so bitterly disappointed when Ewing sent him a copy of the story with a terse note saying he was thinking of giving up the news business to try his hand at fiction. McCrae immediately understood why. The story had been cut to shreds. None of the definitions were used and in their place were 10 crisp paragraphs describing the room, McCrae's disheveled appearance and some comma-strewn quotes about McCrae's ambition to coin a word that would endure beyond his span.

Marty's spirits lifted somewhat when he instantly coined two new words to describe cut-happy editors who were too liberal in their use of punctuation.

"Decrapitated by a commanist," McCrae said, shaking his head.

The mood at the Bolten Museum was changing. Where as people used to bubble with a giddy enthusiasm about being involved in something so historically silly, they were now becoming sort of antsy. They'd exchanged pleasantries, asked some questions, but now it was all about the money, which was today residing in the posh, green-lawned neighborhood of $570 million. They didn't care about McCrae's feelings, what he had to say, or what he thought about the latest political silliness to come from the warring moon territories. Milton Kessler was typical. He and Marty used to talk about kids, baseball, or their mutual contempt for people who preferred cats to dogs. But after a year, he'd walk in, nod hello, and start reading the Daily Racing Form. He was a Manhattan jeweler and an astute gambler to boot. He was pushing 50 and had a rim of crackly gray hair around the temples and a bald, blunt skull that reminded Marty of a .44-caliber slug emerging from a puff of gun barrel smoke. He dressed well, was precise in manner and expression, and Marty asked why he'd clammed up recently.

"'scuse me?" Kessler said.

"I asked why you no longer share your thoughts with me. We used to talk about little things, but it was enjoyable conversation and I looked forward to your visits. Now, you come in more, but say less."

Afternoon sunshine was slicing through the fall clouds and the waning of summer had left Marty feeling melancholy.

"Oh, I'm sorry," Kessler said, not sounding at all sorry. "I didn't mean to be rude. It's just I'm a gambler and I realized you were simply a gambling proposition to me and it didn't make sense to talk to you. I go to the track all the time but you don't hear me asking the horse how its weekend went. And, frankly, I'm starting to resent your longevity."

"Huh?"

"That's right," Kessler said. "You're living way too long. When the doctors said you'd live two, three months tops, it was fun, it was interesting and it was a pleasure to be here with you. But now, for guys like me, you've become a nagging reminder of our obsessions. My wife's to blame, too. She keeps reminding me how much time and money I've spent here just waiting for you to die. She's another kind of nagging reminder, but you know women."

"Ah, no, actually, I don't know women. I've married 'em, loved 'em, been mystified by them - - even shot at by a couple of 'em — but I'd never profess to know women."

"See, that's another thing," Kessler said, seizing on the statement. "You weave these conversations that get my thinking all tangled up. Now, I'll spend the rest of the day thinking about whether or not I really know women. Very distracting. Anyway, my wife thinks you're never going to die. She thinks this is all some kind of government plot to raise money instead of raising taxes. She thinks you really died two years ago and this is an interactive government hologram being used to perpetuate the pot."

"Is she some spooky sort of detective?" McCrae asked.

"No, she's a spooky sort of P.T.A. member. She's got lots of time on her hands. She's always complaining about my gambling. She doesn't like all the time I spend here. I can bet on horses and she never hears about it, but because of your aggressive marketing department, every time I come here she gets a call at home thanking the household for participating, and offering discounts with your sponsors."

"I have nothing to do with those obnoxious tactics," McCrae offered defensively.

"Still, no horse has ever called home to thank our household for betting on it in the fifth at Saratoga."

"Well, why do you keep coming back?" Marty asked. "In fact, our records indicate you used to come by once a month or so, but now you come every week. Twice last week."

"C'mon, Marty, it's the odds. The longer you live, the more likely you'll die."

That was a true fact. Marty'd always said facts were more factual if they were true facts, even though he'd admittedly never seen nor heard anything that could be classified a false fact. Those were simply lies. And a truer fact there'd never been.

They said nothing more during the four minutes that elapsed until Kessler dropped — *ding!* — down the chute.

Nothing, in true fact, ever again during the ensuing 168 times he'd come in with the fervent hope that the old man would die and he'd win back the $19,225 he'd invested and the mega-millions that awaited. Kessler'd zip in and nod at Buster and Marty, unfold his racing form and stand there mute for the next 14 minutes and 59.9 seconds.

Kessler wasn't even the worst. There were 189 players who'd been there more than the 769 times he'd been by. Many of them, too, were professional gamblers who saw his demise as a good bet. They, too, were becoming increasingly angry at McCrae's persistence. One popular website offered hourly updates on symptoms, but the hardcore gamblers never bothered to check it anymore. Like much of the internet, the site was full of false facts and wild distortions about Marty's supposedly failing health. In fact, twice the site had incorrectly predicted that McCrae would die within 2 days, false facts that caused spooky Patti Kessler to tell everyone at the P.T.A. the government was running short of money and needed to inflate the McCrae pool to bail out a fiscal crisis.

But the true gamblers never fell for it. They all knew McCrae never coughed, sneezed, wheezed or had so much as a heart flutter. They knew he was in the pink of health and had the iron constitution of a giant sequoia. Like the trees, he'd withstood hundreds of years of exposure to the elements and was still confounding all the earthly elements. Still, they came, because everyone's got to die someday. Even Marty McCrae.

That was a true fact.

IN DREAMVILLE ...

In what he came to regard as the Dreamville Auditorium, he'd seen just about every important person who'd ever stepped through his life. He was struck by how he and others had glanced off one another and sent their lives in ricochetting in different directions the way the chips did on the Plinko board on the "The Price Is Right." He was reminded of the joy even chance encounters from long ago could hold.

He'd heard the surprising and tender recollections of the girl with whom he shared the loss of their virginities and the felt the sting and spite of those he'd treated badly. His brothers Tom and Judas came by as the teens they were when the three of them brawled and celebrated the joys of just being boys.

Judas complained that it had been Marty's idea to name him after history's worst villain.

"Well, they'd be shoving all the crap down my throat in Sunday school around the time just before you were born," Marty said. "I remember Mr. Lawrence saying Judas was the worst person in history for betraying Jesus."

Marty said how he convinced their father that naming a kid Judas in the 20th century would be doing him an enormous favor. He believed a boy named Judas wouldn't have to do much to exceed expectations. He figured fair-minded evaluators would say, "Naturally, I had my suspicions Judas was going to be a real turncoat, but I find him to be very trustworthy. I recommend we give him a raise. Let's start with 30 pieces of silver and see if he counters."

"Back then, I thought 30 pieces of silver was all the money in the world and to a kid as young as I was then, that seemed incentive enough," Marty said. "Sorry if it caused you any grief."

Judas just smiled. He'd always been a happy, good-hearted kid.

Seeing him and Tom in Dreamville had been a wonderful surprise. He thought he'd had the two best brothers in the world.

And the dreams kept coming. To call them recurrent seemed, to Marty, an understatement. They were tidal. He knew every 12 hours or so when he closed his eyes for even a quick nap he could count on a glorious memory parade, all hosted by Buddy, and spending time with Buddy, any time, seemed a precious gift.

Buddy had been his least talkative, but most intuitive friend. They'd been in perfect synch throughout their lives. That's why Buddy's suicide in 2032 had been so devastating. Marty never saw it coming. No one did. And he couldn't ask him about it

Having dream Buddy so near and so vibrant was a painful tease to dream Marty. He was so near, yet so distant. Protocol seemed to forbid a hug, a question, a conversation with Buddy, who seemed forever too busy with 3 by 5 cards and keeping things moving along in an orderly fashion to engage Marty in any way Marty wished.

But the rest of Dreamville had been a conversational carnival. It was entertaining seeing his life pass before his eyes in this way. He sensed the people to whom he spoke in Dreamville would one day be asked to vote on matters that had only been hinted at, yet it didn't cause dream Marty into kissing any dream ass. He just reacted ~~as he~~ with what to him was abundant honesty that had never been apparent in the world of wide awake Marty.

At least until Brick Ryder took the stage. His appearance gave Marty mixed feelings. He enjoyed seeing Ryder because it reminded him of some of the very best golf he'd ever played. But Ryder was a despicable megalomaniac who'd ruined countless lives. That's what he tried to do to Marty when he marooned him on the planet Gonto. Marty was haunted by the timing of it all.

Had he arrived back on earth just two days earlier, could he have saved Buddy? Would Buddy have called his best friend to talk him out of suicide?

He knew that Ryder had intended for him to die there. As it was, Ryder'd died about one year after he'd dispatched Marty to Gonto, his crimes on earth went unpunished. Marty never did anything about it. No one, he was sure, would have ever believed him.

And he felt protective of the people on Gonto. He could only imagine what the pilgrims would do if they found out there was a planet where Jesus liked to hang. It would ruin Gonto, he knew.

Because no one on Earth knew that Gonto was populated. And no one on Earth knew that Jesus Christ loved to visit there. All they knew, and only a few of them even knew this much, was that corn grew on Gonto and that Gonto looked a lot like Indiana.

And no one on Earth knew that Jesus loved corn or that He would go to the ends of the universe to nibble on a really swell ear.

So things didn't turn out for Marty the way Ryder thought they would. Ryder couldn't have known that Gonto would turn out to be one of the most rich and vibrant experiences in McCrae's century-plus long jaunt through life.

It sure didn't start out that way.

"Whattzis do?" Marty asked.

"Don't touch that."

"T-minus 40 seconds and counting …"

"What'll happen if I push this button?"

"We'll explode."

"How long is this supposed to take?"

"Three months."

"And we're going to be asleep the whole time?"

"Yes, Mr. McCrae."

"Call me Skypilot Martman, please."

"T-minus 35 seconds and counting …"

"Yessir, Skypilot Martman."

"Can I go to the bathroom once more?"

"No."

"It'll be three months before I go to the bathroom again. What if I have an accident?"

"We'll be in suspended animation and we're all wearing bio-diapers, Skypilot Martman."

"Please, can't I go once more? Please! Please!"

"Negatory."

"T-minus 20 seconds and counting …"

"Will you let me steer?"

"This vehicle steers itself, Skypilot Martman. It's remote-controlled from Commander Ryder's lunar base."

"Cool! Whattzis button do?"

"Please, Skypilot Martman, do not, I repeat, do not touch any of the buttons. You are here strictly as an observer at the courtesy of Eminent Commander Ryder. The consequences of your interfering could be substantial. And we could all die."

Ensign Ken Trainor rolled his eyes at Cpl. Tim Novak. What'd they do to deserve this? Of course, he knew what they'd done. They'd pissed off Ryder, the moody son of a bitch. He was blaming them for his being late. They'd arrived to retrieve Ryder and McCrae, er, Skypilot Martman, back from a weekend of galactic golf on Mars. Ryder looked so volcanically angry that Trainor expected lava to flow from his nose. Clearly, Ryder'd lost big. Again. And he was taking his spite out on them. Yeah, being an astronaut was not what they'd anticipated when they were growing up. Back then there was a romance about outer space, and astronauts were heroic, clean-cut figures straight from Greek mythology. The men and women of the space program were souls of daring, skill and wit — if you overlook the dorks who picked the stupid songs they used each morning to wake up the actual astronauts. Each mission was an adventure, every space walk a ballet among the primal frontier.

And then came Bella Luna Resorts, the first private enterprise devoted exclusively to opening up the final frontier to common men and women. Underwritten entirely by Will Ponce and his Virtual Acme Corp., Bella Luna Resorts took huge financial and personal risks to land lunar robots on the Sea of Tranquility. Ponce was roundly vilified as foolhardy and unprepared for the deadly risks when one mission resulted in the death of three interns who were earning minimum wage and engineering course credits for lubricating robots with galactic blasts of WD-40 whenever one of them started to squeak. But it turned out to be a job for seasoned construction workers, not college kids prone to binge drinking and mechanical pranks on lunar robots. Artificial intelligence is a matter of perspective and the lunar robots dispatched the drunken students, perhaps accidentally, when the students, all senior fraternity boys at Purdue, dressed the five robots up like four sorority sisters and one sheep. Their bodies are still exactly as they were, pants down, when the robots turned on them and sent them spinning off through the lonely cosmos. Regardless of the causes, it was a scandal and nearly bankrupted Acme and the personal fortunes accumulated by the company's three founders.

But they persevered. They hired Pittsburgh construction workers, some of the hardiest, toughest men on Earth. They paid them well and gave them strict instructions not to squirt the robots with anything but WD-40.

It worked. And in 2025, five years after the tragedy, Distant Vistas Resort Spa and Casino opened to rave reviews. Junketeering travel writers gushed about the inflatable hotels, the casino, the near-zero gravity basketball courts with their 150-foot high hoops, and how much fun it was to sip Tang Screwdrivers at the karaoke bar while Earth rose off in the great black yonder. Within three years of the opening of Distant Vistas, an inflatable Hooters was opened just down the road from the space port. Then came inflatable churches, T-shirt shacks and a Bob Evans restaurant. Pretty soon, it looked just like Myrtle Beach with all the lights off. Everybody loved it.

Once it had been made to look just like the rest of America, tourists were impatient to go somewhere else. That's when things really took off. Like a rocket. Earth flights to the moon became as common as the old shuttles between New York and Washington.

Astronauts became bus drivers or worse. Even a friendly bus driver can brighten people's days by offering a cheerful, "Morning!" But there was no camaraderie between astronauts and their cargo, as passengers were callously called. For guys like Trainor and Novak, the whole thing was pretty tedious.

They'd been told they were to take Skypilot Martman to Io, the Jupiter moon, to see if conditions were amenable to championship golf. It sounded like a silly sort of mission to Trainor, but he'd do as he was told. As far as space exploration was concerned, Ryder was a demigod. An unquestioned authority responsible for each and every flight as well as its cargo and destination, which meant he was responsible for everything. The moon, despite its gaudy Distant Vistas and other blooming resorts, was becoming little more than a galactic convenience store. Humanity was flourishing across the solar system. It was a truly amazing time to be alive. It just wasn't all that cool to be an astronaut.

"T-minus 15 seconds and counting …"

"I think I forgot my toothbrush!"

"Suspended animation renders daily hygiene unnecessary."

"What about when we get to Io?"

"I have a spare," Novak said helpfully.

"Has it been in anyone's mouth?"

"It has not."

"Will we dream while we're asleep?"

"T-minus 10 … 9 …"

"Studies show dreams do occur in SusAn."

"Susan?"

"Suspended Animation," Novak said. He was really a helpful sort.

"Will we have the same dreams?"

"…8 … 7 …"

"I do not believe that's possible, Skypilot Martman."

"Too bad for you guys. I'm about to embark on a three-month sex dream and it will be out of this world. Get it!"

"Very funny, Skypilot Martman," Trainor said, grateful that he'd soon be pushing the button that induced a three-month sleep in Skypilot Martman. He was sure it would be the longest McCrae would be silent in his entire life. On that point, he was wrong times two.

"…6 … 5 … 4 …"

"Are the girls on Io man-crazy?"

"They are professional researchers and they all have spouses stationed with them," Novak said.

"…3 … 2 …"

"Married! That bites. Who on Earth'd want to have zero-gravity sex with their wife? Lookee, I can see Australia! Hey, whattzis do?"

"…1 … We have liftoff!"

"Don't touch that!"

"Geez, I really need to use the can! Will it be night when we get there? Hey, how big is Jupiter, really? Hey, whattzis do?"

"Don't touch that!"

Trainor violated procedure by deploying Skypilot Martman's SusAn 10 minutes before scheduled. The hell with it. The guy would not shut up. Deep in SusAn for three months, he wouldn't say a peep.

Trainor was sure three months would be the longest he'd ever be silent. He couldn't have known about the coma years at the Bolten museum, and he couldn't have known the black-hearted Brick Ryder had ensured Skypilot Martman would be silent for longer than three months on this mission.

DECEMBER 2030

He awoke on the alien surface of Gonto feeling pudding minded, his nude body shivering from the bracing bucket of water that had been poured over his head. He couldn't have known it at the time, but it had been longer than three months. He and the crew had been in SusAn's womb for 17 months. And it certainly wasn't Io, a Jupiter moon that could be glimpsed from Earth with binoculars. To McCrae, it looked like the Great Midwest, a land sprawling with nondescript landscape as far as the eye could see. Inconceivably, everywhere he looked he saw magnificent, orderly corn stalks spiking straight up out of the ground. It looked like some giant galactic barber had come by and given the entire landscape a crewcut. To him it looked like Io-wa.

The blast from the departing spaceship singed all the hair off his face and head. He saw it circling overhead and began to pitifully yelling after it. "Hey, guys! Where you going? Guys? Come back! What's going on? Are you coming back? Guys! Guys! Guys … guys?"

He watched as the craft slowly, beautifully lifted off the planet and made a long, slow arc until it finally became the invisible end to a long white kite tail into a cerulean blue sky.

Even in his confusion, he marveled at its beauty. He couldn't have known that his flight had lasted, not 3 months, but a year and a half. Nor could he have known that Trainor and Novak had dithered for a day trying to decide if they had any option but to follow the landing orders that required them to deposit McCrae's still slumbering body, revive him with a dousing bucket of cold water, and then surreptitiously scram for home and another three solitary years alone with SusAn.

Ryder, who'd be found dead of natural causes upon their return, had exiled McCrae to the far reaches of outer space, to a place known to support plant life and nothing else. McCrae could not have known this as he stood staring at the blue sky for maybe an hour as the rocket's glare faded to nothing. Just a big, empty blue sky above a tabletop abundant with green corn ripening in the sunshine.

Then … drifting down from the blue he noted a parachute descending rapidly to the surface. An explanation? Supplies? Distress signals? Had to be! He trudged in frustrating circles for nearly six hours through the fresh, unending sea of corn before finally finding the billowing parachute. Beneath its tethered strings was a cushioned package about the size of a Brady Bunch lunch box he'd had as a kid. He unwrapped the protective casing, the bubble wrap interior and scattered the peanut packing to uncover the contents. Inside was a shaker of salt, a stick of butter, two corn-on-the-cob holders and a package of mint-flavored dental floss.

There were no birds. No mice. No groundhogs. There were no roads, no farm equipment, no farmers, no tractors, no silos jutting into the clear blue sky. Just corn. Rows and rows and rows of corn clear to the horizon. In his endless wandering, he tried in vain to think of an appropriate metaphor. More ears than at a teeming Chinese soccer stadium. More ears per square inch than at an elephant orgy. More ears than … ah, it was just really a lot of corn.

He ate about 25 ears a day for nearly a week and the first five ears were really, truly delicious. But those were just five ears out of more than 150. About the sixth one, he started getting really sick of corn — even the best corn — and he was reminded not for the last time of the saying about about how even the guy who's screwing the world's most beautiful woman eventually tires of the repetition.

Divine repetition. Would it have been so bad if it had been, say, a banana planet? A bananet, he supposed they'd call it. He loved bananas, but they, too, would have made him sick after the first bunch or so. Or peanuts? He used to love eating peanuts in the bleachers at baseball games but then he decided they were too hard to open so he quit cold turkey. A cold turkey planet? A room temperature turkey planet? That might have some advantages. Maybe he could alternate eating a couple and training a couple until he could entertain himself with a turkey circus.

No matter. Anything that repetitive would drive him crazy. He was sure. He was so sure he was going to lose his mind in the maize maze he actually began to anticipate it with some relief. It would, indeed, be a fine madness. He figured he wasn't on Io. He would have heard about all the corn. He'd been told to expect mind-bending vistas filled with of volcanos spewing poison gas. A hell of a place.

And he could have constructed a really fine golf course there, he was sure. Golfers, essentially a sissy bunch, loved to feel a rush of danger. Here, among the corn, there would be no danger. No sense of urgency. He supposed he could uproot a few hundred yards of corn and make a fairway, but it would be pockmarked and crappy and an exceedingly difficult place from which to play a shot. It would be an unfairway.

But even that wouldn't abate the onset of lunacy. It never occurred to him that Ryder was behind the whole thing. If he'd have thought Ryder had willfully seen to his dispatch, that would have made him instantly crazy and it wouldn't have been a pretty crazy. It would have been a frothing, roaring, gibberish of lunacy. He assumed the insanity that awaited him would be the kind where you lie on your back and stare up at the sky as your mind turns to one big marshmallow. He liked marshmallows.

A marshmallow planet? That's one he thought he could enjoy. Nothing but marshmallows or maybe Easter Peeps. It would be wonderful. Sure, a diet of nothing but marshmallows would rot away his teeth in a few quick months, but what do you need teeth for if all you're doing is gumming down mounds of marshmallows? And sleep would be more comfortable, too, on a marshmallow landscape. He hadn't slept at all well during the nights among the corn stalks. But that wasn't so bad, either, because he was fascinated by the new sky above him. Not only could he see two moons — two! — but there was a fresh splash of stars dotting the blackness, and he enjoyed conceiving his own stellar constellations and naming them after famous pornographic movie actresses. There was Topaz the Acrobat; Spanking Sara; Double-Jointed Gina; and AleXXX the Naughty, which required a writhing string of 15 celestial bodies. These were truly some porn stars.

Even with the fitful sleep, the nights weren't all that bad. But the days were dreadful. Monotonous, circular treks through the corn. He may as well have been going in circles. He left no trail. The corn seemed to swallow up his past as surely as it would consume his future. Knee high by the Fourth of July. If that was the case, he judged it was like July 25 because the corn was up clear past his neck. It was everywhere. From sea to shining sea, but without the seas. Just corn and more corn. Corn, corn, corn, corn, corn, corn, corn … and then a little one-armed man toting what appeared to be a corn-studded gift basket.

"Greetings, Earthling! My name is dy Ego. Welcome to Gonto. Here, have some of our delicious corn in case you're hungry."

He had no right arm and his skin had the same orangish complexion cultivated by the super-wealthy residents of Palm Beach, Florida. He looked as if they've been immersed in Tang, and that's what this gently smiling fellow looked like, too. Tang Man. He could take him, he was sure, but he tired easily these days and had not the vigor for combat, especially since he was fully nude. Nude Earth men make poor warriors, he felt.

Tang Man told Marty he'd gone to Gonto. It was a planet, sailing around a cozy little star about three light years from the near side of the Betelgeusean solar system.

"Gonto?"

"You didn't know?"

"Uh, no," Marty said, feeling somewhat unsophisticated, like a hick tourist. "They told me they were taking me to Io, a moon just off the southern end of Jupiter."

dy Ego let go a bark of laughter. "Io! My friend, you've been badly misled. You are roughly 1.7 trillion of your Earth miles from Io. You are on the planet Gonto and are a long, long way from home. But, fear not, we have an Earth-bound shuttle departing early next week. We'll see to your care until then and you'll be free to go. I must say, however, you might enjoy spending a little time on Gonto. We grow really great corn. Much better than Earth's. Just ask Jesus."

Marty stopped dead in his tracks. "Did you say Jesus?"

"Yes, in fact, in the entire history of Gonto, you and Jesus are the only aliens to ever have even bothered to set foot on Gonto. Most galactic tourists, the ones with even the capacity to observe us, believe a place with this much corn must be boring, you know, like the place you Earthlings call Indiana."

"I'm sorry, I'm not sure I'm following you. You did say Jesus?"

"Yeah, in fact, you just missed Him by a couple of days. Great guy. His birthday's coming up, you know? You should stick around for that. It's very traditional."

"Jesus Christ?"

"That's him."

"He was here?"

"Yes, He was."

"Jesus Christ!"

"That's the one."

"Jesus Christ the Lord?"

"The one and only."

"Jesus Christ!"

"Now I can't tell if that's praise or profanity."

"Jesus Christ! Do you know who He is?"

"He's our savior. Yours, too. He's the greatest. He's here all the time. He loves it here."

"Are you telling me, Jesus Christ the Lord comes here just … just … just to visit?"

"Well, he comes by every once in a while, maybe every couple of months or so just to check in and see how we're all doing. Let me tell you, when Jesus visits, the place comes to a complete stop. Nobody works, the streets are empty. We just sit around listening to Him talk. And, man, can that guy talk. Just get Him started and He'll go all day. If it was anybody else, you might be kind of put off by it, Him talking all the time. But, after all, this is Jesus. I'm telling you, He's the greatest."

Marty was dumbfounded.

"It's been more than 2,000 years since he's been to Earth," Marty moaned. "And He just stops in here all the time just to shoot the breeze?"

"He enjoys riding a bicycle around the planet, too," he said and smiled contentedly while Marty tingled with excitement. He was walking in the steps — or perhaps the bicycle tire tracks — of the Lord. And it wasn't like Israel or the Holy Land. Here, on this strange little planet, the tracks were still fresh. He asked if they regularly prayed to Jesus for His help.

"I don't know whether you call it prayer, really, we just ask Him. Sometimes, some of the children will ask questions like, 'Hey, Jesus, can you make me taller?' Or once we had a guy come right out and say, 'Jesus Christ, my wife won't get off my back. Can you do something about her bitching?' He won't do something like that, but He'll give you a good answer. Understand most people here would never ask for something like that. We're a very contented people but if, say, your mother has gout and her foot's acting up and you ask Him to heal it, He'll usually do something about it. He's very cool and he doesn't like to see people suffer needlessly."

Gout. His own mother had suffered a painful bout of gout, and Marty felt a surge of resentfulness. Why hadn't Jesus answered his prayers to ease the suffering of his own dear mother? He admitted his feelings to dy Ego and asked how come He never visits Earth.

"Well, let's be honest, you guys didn't treat Him so good last time. I mean the crucifixion and all. Nothing like that's ever happened to Him here. In fact, we're just overjoyed to have Him around. But, hey, I have some good news for you! He's planning on coming back to Earth in, let's see, He said around 2083. How do you like them apples!"

Marty, who'd just spent his 63rd birthday lost amid the Gonto corn, did the math in his head. It took a while before he responded with caustic sarcasm.

"Oh, that's just great. It won't do me much good. It's not like I'm going to live to be, what, 119 years old?"

"I am sorry," dy Ego said, sounding genuinely so. "Meeting Him's amazing. He's like a God around here. What am I talking about? He IS God around here. The son of God, but that's sort of splitting hairs, don't you think?"

"Well, why here? What's so great about this place that He comes here all the time? What makes you guys so damned special that Jesus Christ the Lord just stops by every so often just … just … just … to chat."

"Jesus loves corn."

Marty did not like corn. That was just one of the ways in which he and Jesus differed. Still, that dietary dilemma didn't dampen his enthusiasm for meeting the Lord. Right there, he impetuously vowed to spend on Gonto as much time as it took for him to get to break bread with Jesus. Or more likely nibble an ear with Him.

He learned that Earth had been an abiding passion for Gontoians for the past 150 years, back when they mastered intergalactic travel and a cunning self-preservational ability to conceal their villages from prying telescopic eyes. They were light years ahead of Earth in that they could travel to the farthest reaches of the universe in a matter of days.

dy Ego told him Earth fascinated extraterrestrials because of its beauty, its diversity and its inhabitants' competing passions for love and violence. It made for great entertainment, he said.

dy Ego confessed, too, to some embarrassing excesses of their Earth field trips, mostly tabloid-type fables that had, indeed, been based in reality. True, Gontoians had abducted Earthlings for research purposes. True, they had conducted experiments on them. True, they had inserted tiny tracking devices in the fatty excesses of their bulging buttocks. And, true, they had used sophisticated probes to examine the anal canals of some terrified Earthlings.

"What did you do with them once you had conducted your experiments," he asked dy Ego.

"Oh, we had to get rid of them. They were useless. Smelled bad, too. So we simply destroyed them all."

A cold chill dashed up Marty's spine. "You mean to tell me that once you'd conducted your experiments on these innocent men and women, you just got rid of them?" Could

166

this amiable alien really be so cold-blooded about the taking of a human life?

"What? No! Oh, you're mistaken. I thought you were talking about the probes. We got rid of the probes. The people we just returned to Earth unharmed. No biggie."

When they got to the little village where the people of Gonto lived, Marty was treated like a king, in fact. Not the King of Kings, but a king nonetheless. He'd enter a tavern and half expect applause to break out and instinctively reached out to shake the hands of every single person he met and never quite got the hang of retracting it without some awkwardness. It dawned on him that Gonto was a place where no one, not even Jesus Christ, would ever hear applause.

All they had were left limbs.

An entire planet of disabled people. A race of people born without their right arms.

Marty thought quietly, "Man, I wish Skip could get a load of this."

They were the most contented people he'd ever met. They ate corn three meals a day, every day and never got tired of it. The fashions never changed. They were strictly monogamous. Marriages lasted a lifetime and lifetimes lasted nearly 350 years.

Their soul secular extravagance was travel. They reveled in voyages across the universe, but to Earth in particular. Earth was their idea of heaven. They believed a contented and good life on Gonto would be rewarded with a safer version of Earth in heaven.

In fact, all the Earth-Gonto shuttles had the call letter prefix of HCW, an abbreviation for "Heaven Can Wait."

So Marty wasn't at all surprised to learn there had never been a single instance of suicide on Gonto. Ever. It was a statistic Marty could salute. He'd known a handful of suicides in his day and had usually reacted to their ends with bitter scorn. The taking of one's own life for any reason seemed a heartless sacrilege, the desperate province of the stupid and the weak.

He'd suffered humiliation, poverty, despair, heartbreak, and had never once considered ending it all. Why should he? He was convinced the world was too ripe with laughter and love that more wouldn't blossom somewhere when some of his began to wilt. He'd laugh the hardest when things got really bad. He couldn't wait to see if they could possibly get any worse. Usually, they did not. When you hit rock bottom, there's no where to go but up. And he'd hit bottom so many times he'd developed saddle-like callouses on his buttocks. Humiliation's only humiliating for those who've never learned to laugh at themselves. He'd mastered that years ago. He reveled in his foibles, follies and foolish mistakes.

Poverty only means poor when you're comparing yourself to the wrong people. He'd been dumpster-diving broke a number of times in his life, but that always made him recall the poor souls who lived and died among the trash dumps in the Philippines. He'd ~~heard~~ once heard that 30 people died while sifting through a mountain of trash at the dump where they made their home. Then the trash caught on fire. He wondered for weeks without resolution what they did with the bodies. Do you bury them in a cemetery? Being dead in a cemetery must have been better than living in a landfill. He'd been penniless many times after that and never felt poor when he thought of the poor, damned Filipino trash people.

He reserved his most blazing contempt for heartbreak suicides. That any woman or man could feel so in love with another person that their departure would cause them to end their lives was beyond his comprehension. He'd seen too many marriages bust up only to find passable happiness with another. Love was disposable, or at least transferrable. There are lots of fish in the sea. Marty thought the important thing was making sure his rod was always ready.

❦

He stayed two years before deciding it was time to go home. During that time, Jesus never showed. dy Ego said after the first year it was the longest He'd ever stayed away, and some of them began to wonder if His absence had something to do with Marty's presence, but no one believed that. Most just felt Jesus was probably busy somewhere and told Marty not to feel too bad about it. Still, Marty decided he missed home too much to spend the rest of his life just waiting around for Jesus. Plus, he was sick and tired of corn and had been really craving a good cheeseburger. The Gontoian contentment was not infectious.

He'd loved being on Gonto and until the day he died, he considered his days there among the best of his entire life. He felt a real kinship with the tiny people and they returned his affections many times over.

"Well, why don't you stay?" dy Ego asked.

"I miss my friends on Earth and there's no place like home."

169

"Wrong. There's no place like Earth. We'd leave Gonto in a minute if we could move to Earth, but you'd all probably kill us. You'd be afraid because we're different."

Marty wasn't going to argue that one.

Shuttle HCW 925 was leaving in 15 minutes and it was a festive atmosphere at the terminal where the commodious space ship was being readied for flight. About 20 Gontoians were mingling about with loved ones and they were dressed up in disguises and costumes that made Earth Halloween seem as tame as a kindergarten candy swap. They loved to dress up. Whole herds of them would pose in Times Square for pictures as busy New Yorkers hurried by, never realizing they were steps away from a platoon of galactic tourists. The thought made Marty smile at how jaded New Yorkers could be.

He'd been looking forward to the flight as eagerly as he'd been looking forward to getting home. Gonto ran its space ships much better than Earth airlines. There was room to walk around, a spacious jacuzzi & spa, a lively polka band and flights so smooth passengers could actually play billiards.

dy Ego gave him one last warm, one-armed embrace, and Marty felt tears come to his eyes. "Don't cry, my friend!" dy Ego said, laughing. "We've enjoyed a friendship that's unique to the universe and I'll never forget you."

"Will I ever see you again?"

"Tomorrow is promised to no one, but who knows? We'll keep an eye out for you."

"I'll miss you."

"And I will miss you. But our tests indicate you will have every opportunity to live long and prosper. And we'll keep tabs on you."

"Tests? Tabs? You guys didn't put a chip in my butt to monitor my whereabouts, did you?"

"Marty!" he laughed. "What do you take us for? You're our friend. We would never resort to such intrusive and distasteful methods with someone we treasure as much as we treasure you."

He apologized. He supposed dy Ego was just speaking metaphorically and he felt a rash of shame steal across his soul.

"Now, what are you going to do once you get back to Earth?"

"I think I'll get another dog, name it Rex, and try to round up some of my old friends."

He looked around and for the last time drank in the strange surroundings. Earth-like, but so alien. "Most of all, I think I'd like to track down my old friend Buddy. Now, there's a guy you'd get along with. He's the most fun-loving Earthling there is."

"Buddy? What's his last name?"

"Buddy Allman."

"Buddy Allman? I think we can find him for you." He began pecking away at a nearby keyboard.

"Oh, I don't think so. He's a rambling sort. He may be impossible to find, even for me."

"Ah, good! Here you go," he said, handing him a print out. "He's in Darwin, Minnesota. He's been there for the past five years, four months and twenty three days."

"Darwin, Minnesota? What on Earth would he be doing there? There's nothing there. It's the home to the world's largest ball of twine. I had my picture taken there when I was traveling with the carnival one year."

Then he became suddenly suspicious at the easy locating of rambling Buddy. "And just how do you guys know he's in Darwin, Minnesota?"

"We found him drunk in a hedge about 40 years ago and picked him up for observation," dy Ego said. "And then we put a chip in his butt."

FEBRUARY 2032

He landed with a thud less than a mile east of Darwin. It was February and the bitter winds were enjoying a 1,500-mile unobstructed prairie run off the Canadian Rockies before they could instantly pinken any foolishly exposed cheek with the bitchslap ferocity of a scorned lover. He began briskly walking west. The first human being he'd seen in nearly three years looked from a distance little different than the one-armed aliens he'd befriended on Gonto.

It was Skip. He stood stamping his feet against the cold outside the Klipstein LaPlant & Sons Funeral Home directly across the street from the Twine Ball Inn, cater corner from the Twine Ball Restaurant and just a block down the street from the late Francis Johnson's 11-ton ball of twine, a national landmark for eccentric road warriors.

What Skip was doing standing outside a funeral home in godforsaken Darwin, Minnesota, Marty had no idea. What Marty was doing sauntering up in a purple sweat suit, sneakers and a Tang orange tan in the middle of a Minnesota winter, Skip had no idea.

"Where the hell have you been?" Skip demanded.

"You wouldn't believe me if I told you."

"Well, I'm glad you got the message. I kept telling everyone you'd be here. Did he try and call you? Did he try and get in touch?"

Marty was baffled by the conversation, disoriented by the strange buzz he was getting from the Earth oxygen, and he was starting to lose feeling in his toes. "What message?" He hadn't seen Skip in six years and his friend was showing his age. He was bald on the dome with a fringe of salt and pepper hair horseshoeing around the temples and back. He looked like he needed a warm bath and a long nap. His bloodshot eyes searched out Marty's soul.

"You don't know, do you?"

"Know what? What are you talking about?"

Skip was the toughest of them all. The loss of an arm hadn't fazed him. He'd still gone through life with both guns blazing, no small metaphorical feat for a one-armed man. He was analytical, daring, unafraid and reckless with his life and the feelings of others. When Skip began to weep, Marty began to feel woozy.

"Dear God, you don't know," he said. "Buddy's dead."

He threw his arm around Marty and began to sob on his shoulder.

"Dead? That can't be. They told me he was here. They said he was living in Darwin."

"Who told you? Where the hell have you been?"

Marty's mind reeled. He ignored Skip's question and responded with one of his own.

"How?"

"Ah, Marty, it was a suicide. He blew his brains out. He took a gun, sat down by the fireplace in his cabin, lit a candle, drank a glass of cheap red wine and then blew his brains out all over the hearth."

Grief would come later, he figured. After, oh, what was it? Acceptance? Was that it? Or was it anger? He was having trouble thinking. Was it anger, then acceptance, then grief? Or was it the other way around? He didn't know, but he knew he was starting from square one. The first step loss counselors always said in the event of a sudden, inexplicable loss was denial. Marty embraced it and was happy to be playing by the rules.

"Noooo …" he said in slow disbelief. Marty was absolutely certain there must have been some mistake. Buddy would never kill himself. He was too strong. "You and I know Buddy of all people would never kill himself."

"Goddamn it, Marty! Don't be such an idiot. I identified the body. He's got a friggin' hole in the side of his head. He blew half his face away. Don't come waltzing in here and tell me he's not dead. I've been through too much this weekend to have to put up with that crap."

Skip had the anger phase down pat.

"Dead?"

"Dead."

"Suicide?"

"Suicide."

"Buddy?"

"Yeah, Buddy."

It was starting to sink in. But suicide? No way. He wasn't weak. He wasn't a quitter. He loved life too much to take his own.

"Did he have any enemies? You and I know he couldn't kill himself. He wouldn't. He's not one of those sorry bastards. Not Buddy."

Skip's tears were stemming. He sobbed once more and began to compose himself with one last sniffle salute. "It was a suicide."

"C'mon," he shook his head again, slowly, uncomprehendingly. "It could have been staged."

"He left a note. I saw it."

"A suicide note?"

"It was simple, right to the point. Just like Buddy. No bull. He just said what he had to say. Then he pulled the trigger."

"Well, what did it say?"

"It said, 'Goodbye cruel world.' That's it. Three little words, then, BANG! Dead."

Marty seized on the last ray of hope he'd ever feel in regards to the demise of the man whose death by his own hand would haunt him the remainder of his days.

"Hey! The note could have been faked! He could have had some enemies that came in, shot him, and then written the note and left it to make it look like a suicide. Three words! That wouldn't be too hard to fake!"

"This was authentic. I verified it for the police myself. Believe me. It was pure Buddy."

"How can you be so sure?"

"Two of the three words were misspelled."

"No! Nooo!!! Noooooooo!!! Nooooo …"

Now it was Marty's turn to sob. He'd raced from denial to acceptance in near record time.

There's nothing like the funeral of a suicide. Questions hang in the air like Christmas ornaments, each one begging to be examined and turned over and over in a shiny, surreal light.

Why? How? What was he thinking? Couldn't he have called someone? Will scandal emerge? Could it have been a mistake? Was there a secret sickness? Am I to blame? Dear God almighty, could any of this have been my fault?

Marty immediately lashed out at Ryder and vowed to kill him. It was his fault, he was sure, that he was marooned on Gonto for what may have been Buddy's death spiral. Had he been home he felt sure Buddy would have reached out and just as certain that he'd have had some answers for him. Marty was furious when he found out Ryder'd been dead for six months and he couldn't kill him.

Marty'd heard that suicide is a period at the end of a long sentence that no one ever bothered to read. Was Buddy ever trying to tell him something? Was there a sadness concealed in his laughter, a laughter infectious enough to make strangers smile on a bus?

He'd already been married twice and swore to everyone he'd never marry again. He'd told that, too, to the girl with whom he'd been living for the past five years. She was Heather Holsupple and together they were perfect. Heather had had a crazy old aunt who lived on a farm near Darwin. Heather moved from Minneapolis to Darwin to care for the aunt after the police called to say she'd driven her tractor up the steps of the Darwin Public Library. Heather took the tractor and the aunt and put them both back where they belonged. She met Buddy in an Internet chat room where he was trying to pick up lonely women caring for loved ones stricken with Alzheimer's. He'd even invented a crazy old aunt of his own he called Mabel. She was a real mess and he was glad he killed her off the day Heather typed that she was leaving her own aunt with her sister to come visit Buddy in Florida. He typed back that she'd just died and he'd love to see her because he really needed a break.

He was so taken with Heather he moved to Darwin to help her care for her Aunt Rebecca. He opened a crappy little bait shop and fell madly and happily in love with Heather. When Aunt Rebecca died one fine spring morning, it was Buddy who stepped forward and took care of all the arrangements down at Klipstein LaPlant & Sons Funeral Home where he made friends with loquacious funeral director Ralph LaPlant, who told Buddy all the great funeral director jokes and stories he'd heard over the years.

LaPlant was very fond of Buddy and told Heather not to blame herself for his suicide. No one blamed her. At least not to her face. It had to be someone's fault. Things don't just happen. Not in life. And not in the ending of life.

The casket was closed. In hindsight, everyone agreed it probably should have been sealed with industrial rubber bands. Something, anything to clamp it tighter than a doomed lobster's snap-snap-snapping claws seconds after the crustacean takes the boiling plunge.

Skip spent 10 minutes in the snow vainly consoling — "There, there …" — the inconsolable Marty McCrae. He should have skipped the funeral entirely and taken him straight to the Twine Ball Inn for drinks, but instead he took him inside to hear Reverend Noreen Friested eulogize a man she'd never met.

She talked about his warmth. His joy. His fellowship and his dedication to his fellow man. She talked about his tireless efforts on behalf of kidney transplant patients who were living longer, fuller lives because he'd spearheaded lifesaving pop tab collection drives. In tribute, the funeral home had placed two enormous bins at the head of the coffin so donors could deposit their collections right near Buddy's body. Beer drinking was encouraged during the services, too, so pop tabs could be accumulated. *Ka-plushh!* sounds routinely rang out during the eulogy. She held one of the simple shiny metal openers up from the pulpit and thrust it toward heaven.

"This is the legacy of Buddy Allman!" she exalted. "It's a simple, utilitarian device. Something most of us take for granted. Not Buddy. In this, he recognized a way to help his fellow man."

Marty looked around the room. Every one of the fifty or so people seemed to be holding a container of pop tabs. Some just a cupful. Others held boxes the size of milk crates. These were from the various community or office drives Buddy had sponsored.

On the aging faces of his friends, he saw tears. An impenetrable sadness hung like heavy winter coats. Marty'd never drunk a beer during a funeral, but it had never been encouraged as a civic duty before Buddy's goodbye. *Ka-plushh!* Good thing who ever set this shindig up didn't drink bottle beer. It would have been cruelly indifferent to deprive all the sick kids of the 40 or so precious minutes the pop tabs would realize, he thought sarcastically as he scanned the room.

There was Buddy's sister Eileen, her husband Mitch and the 10-year-old twin grandchildren, Sean and Caitlin, they'd been raising since cervical cancer had robbed the kids of their single mother. Mitch, who'd been fishing pals with Buddy, looked catatonic until he'd glance down at the fidgeting twins. He couldn't very well tell them their great uncle wasn't feeling well and blew a hole in his head. Hunting accident sounded about right. It'd be best for the kids.

Will was sobbing like a baby. He'd been zeroed in on trying to get people to live forever and it stunned him that one of his best friends wasn't going to be around for the first drug trials he was sure would come one day soon. He'd been an ardent capitalist all his life, but he'd never once marketed a drug whose potential side effects had included suicidal thoughts. That made Acme Pharmaceuticals a singular rarity among drug manufacturers who considered suicide a by-product of tinkering with biomechanics of the human psyche. It just came with the territory.

Marty was always struck by the etiquette of a funeral. It was a like a party designed to be no fun. It pained him that he was in a room with 50 people bound by a love for Buddy and they couldn't revel in it. Swapping stories would be wrong, giggling forbidden. No one, he was sure, was going to ask any of the kids if they wouldn't mind pulling their finger.

It was the first time in his life he was in the same room with these people where the chances of laughter were absolute zero. He'd enjoyed eruptions of inappropriate laughter with each of them before. Inappropriate laughs were sometimes the sweetest. The problem here was the giggles usually commenced from Buddy and now aching despair was the prevailing sentiment of everyone in the room, excepting the Reverend Friested, who was doing her best to cheerlead the mourners into believing Buddy's death enjoyed a purpose.

"We can use this loss as a beacon for gain," she said. "His death need not be in vain."

Marty looked at Skip and rolled his eyes. Skip stared numbly at the floor.

"And when you deposit your pop tabs into the collection banks we have set up beside the grave, remember that each one is, in fact, life itself. You're contributing to the life that Buddy — for whatever reason — chose to end. His life is over, but his lessons are not. Each of these pop tabs — and there must be thousands of them, maybe a year's worth — are minutes that will prolong the lives of those who want desperately to live the minutes Buddy forfeited. Let that be Buddy's monument. Let us pray . . ."

Marty tapped Skip on the shoulder. "Let's get the hell out of here."

Skip looked at him the way a gardener looks at a weed. "Shhh!!! We're trying to pray here."

"You're buying this?"

"I'm just thinking of Buddy. You should, too."

He'd had enough of hearing how Buddy gave up his own minutes for the minutes of strangers in some fairy tale recycling exchange that made suicide sensible. He hadn't been drunk since he left the moon and a forgotten thirst began pounding at a tiny door inside his head. He would let it in.

"Gimme $20."

Skip reached into his wallet. "Here's $50. Go have yourself a party. The rest of us are going to go bury Buddy."

"Thanks. I'll have one for you. And one for Buddy."

Friested concluded, " …in Jesus' name, we pray."

⁓≫≪⁓

Why February? In Minnesota? So many questions, but those were the two most of the freezing Floridians were thinking as they stepped outside the funeral home and hurried into the flagged cars waiting to drive them to the cold, gray cemetery.

Skip crowded into the big limo with the Ponces and Kimbles. They drove the rest of the way in stony silence, except for when Mitch tried to reassure the kids everything would be fine, that they'd be back in the hotel soon, and that they could order a pizza and maybe go for a walk on a frozen lake.

Yeah, then everything would be fine, Skip thought. Sure. Of course, he couldn't have known just how many questions these bright young kids would have within an hour. They'd buried their mother two years earlier when they were 8. Their sweet sadness at her funeral was touching to all. Here, they'd acted mostly bored and confused. Sure, they remembered the man they called "Pull My Finger Buddy." He was the lovable uncle who gave them candy and always made them laugh. The closed casket had confused them, and had greatly disappointed Sean, who was ghoulishly eager to see a dead body before the day was over.

The skeletal oaks and maples clattered their branches in the wind like gently applauding patrons welcoming actors to a stage upon their approach. The preacher stood bundled against the wind beside the grave. LaPlant, the funeral director stood next to her talking in the hushed, practiced tones of his profession. Off in the distance, but not nearly out of eyesight or earshot, a John Deere back hoe rumbled. It had cut the ground that would hold Buddy's moldering remains from now till the end of time. Two gravediggers stood with cupped hands lighting menthol cigarettes for one another. They'd already planted two bodies that day and were looking forward to heading out to the reservation casinos and strip clubs where they tried to impress strippers by telling them they were minor league baseball players. They thought this would make them hornier than telling them they were gravediggers at the local bone yard. Either way, the strippers didn't care. Gravedigger, ballplayer, doctor, it was still $20 a lap dance.

Skip, Mitch, Will, Marty, Heather's brother Brad and a stout neighbor named Hank were supposed to bear the pall. Bear the pall, Skip thought. Isn't that what pallbearer implied? Six of them ought to be enough, but Skip was sure this pall was unbearable, especially since it looked like Marty was blowing it off.

They were one bearer of pall shy. LaPlant learned of this and said, sure, he'd do it. He'd born plenty of pall. His life was all about pall. In fact, he'd toyed with the idea of renaming his funeral home the Klipstein LaPlant & Sons Pall Mall because, after all, that's what it was. Each room was a pall. He'd done it all his life, ever since he'd begun working for his dad, so he was sure he could bear one more pall.

Skip slid out of the limo and worked the glove onto his left hand, pulled it snug with his teeth, and braced himself against the cold. He'd be glad when this was over.

The six of them gathered around the hearse and nodded to one another. "Gentlemen, let's get this done and be careful," LaPlant said. "The ground's frozen in spots. Let's go slow and easy. Slow and easy."

They nodded, took their positions around the gurney holding the coffin and — one! two! three! — heaved it up. At the time of his death, Buddy weighed 198 pounds, about 25 less than he'd weighed earlier in the year before he and Heather had embraced some stupid cabbage soup diet. Skip felt the strain on his shoulder and was grateful Buddy had shed the pounds before he'd shed the blood. Still, if he was going to do it, it would have been better if he'd have done it in another couple of months. It would have been warmer, Buddy would have probably weighed about 185 or so and, who knows, maybe something would have happened where he'd have been talked out of ending his life. That would have been really great.

LaPlant was right. The walking was tough. Each was wearing formal dress shoes and the leather soles made precarious traction on the astroturf walkway that led from the paved road to the neatly carved hole in front of the gray, granite tombstone starkly engraved with:

Buddy Allman
Nov. 3, 1962 - Feb. 15, 2032

Simple. Straight to the point. They took the coffin to the vicinity of the thick blue straps that would be used to lower Buddy into the ground. The casket, which looked to Skip like a big, shiny oaken bullet, hovered above the hole as a hush-voiced LaPlant directed them to — "Easy, easy …" — set it down in place.

Boom!

In the distance they heard what sounded like a rifle shot. Everyone jumped a little. Just when the nerves settled — *Boom!* — there it was again. Closer.

"Now, pay attention," LaPlant said with a bit of urgency. "We need to take two steps back … Easy … easy …"

Lactic acid was pouring into Skip's arm. He was becoming an old man. The arm that used to be as strong as any two was fatiguing more easily these days. Still, it was strong enough to support the end near Buddy's head. Weakness wasn't the reason he would be dropping it. No, that would have been because of Marty. A third report, this time like a cannon shot — *Boom!* — signaled the entrance of a battered, primer-black Chevy S-10 pickup truck roaring around the bend of the county cemetery road, smoking like a locomotive. LaPlant, who wasn't paying attention to his pall bearing duties anymore, recognized it to be the souped-up vehicle of Bobby Skerlach, who was always pestering him to buy him booze whenever he found him walking into Red's Liquors, Spirits, Beers, Cigs 'n' Chips two blocks down from Twine Ball Hall. LaPlant was an abstemious man and he had no need for any of Red's advertised products. But he did like to wager once in a while and Red was also the town bookie. LaPlant would never consider buying hootch for an underage child, especially for one of the Skerlach children. He'd already buried five Skerlachs and, he hated to admit it, he couldn't bury the rest of them fast enough. They were trouble. So much trouble, in fact, that he scarcely noticed Marty McCrae riding like a cowboy water skier atop the truck's bed, clutching the frozen roll bar with one hand and a half-empty fifth of Jack Daniel's sipping whiskey in the other.

Everyone seemed hypnotized by the black truck and its oddly chipper passengers. Marty spryly hopped out the back, went around the front and gave Skerlach a warm salute. Skerlach returned it with smiling thumb's up, shoved the truck into gear and then — *Boom!* — backfire cracked loud enough to scatter three doe that had been foraging near the edge of the cemetery about two dozen stones over.

It was loud enough, in fact, to startle Skip's aching arm into losing its grip. Loud enough to startle all the pallbearers. The pall fell. So did the casket containing the last Earthly remains — at least all the remains they could scrape off the bloodstained Earth — onto the ground. Skip's edge, Buddy's left front, hit first. Luckily, no one had been paying attention to the procedural faux pas, least of all LaPlant, who couldn't wait to bury that little Skerlach bastard and was hoping to God he outlived him by at least two dozen years. The coffin wasn't properly situated over the precise hole carved by the bored, horny gravediggers. It was askew, a cockeyed coffin. It fell with Buddy's left heel resting above the southwest corner and what remained of his right ear listening off to the northeast. Had it fallen straight onto the blue straps, it might have landed with sufficient force to send the whole works straight to the bottom of the grave and the whole subsequent fiasco might have been averted, or at least resulted in a different sort of fiasco.

The coffin fell with sufficient force to jar the lid loose, and the unseemly disruption convinced Friested it was time to get this show on the road, this coffin in the ground. She made some brief remarks, then asked everyone to bring forth their lifesaving containers that would be distributed to kidney dialysis patients, transplant survivors, and any number of stricken souls who'd benefit from the pop tabs.

One by one, the mourners stood up and poured their hundreds of pop tabs into the container marked "Buddy's Buddies." Skip looked back at Marty, who was hovering on the edge of the 40 mourners who stood in the chill awaiting their turn.

Ka-plushhh!!! Marty popped open a Rolling Rock. He drained it in one quick gulp. He gave an involuntary little shudder and turned and let out a loud belch that was audible to everyone above the ground at the cemetery. He worked the tab back and forth until it broke off.

Not 20 feet away, a downpour of pop tabs sounded like spring rains on a tin roof as mourners walked past the receptacle at the head of the coffin. There were thousands of them. Tens of thousands. Minutes. Hours. Weeks. Months. Maybe years. A whole calendar of calories.

Ka-plushhh!!! Marty opened a second, tore the tab off and set the first empty on top of the hearse that had brought Buddy and Heather and some of their grieving relatives to the cemetery. It looked like he'd intended it to stay there like a Green Hornet sort of siren, but one gust of crackling wind took care of that. The empty can went clattering down the front windshield, off the hood and rolling onto the grass where it desecrated the grave of a beer-swigging World War

II veteran who really wouldn't have minded having a Rock leaning against his rock.

Ka-plushhh!!! Three. Skip hadn't seen him chug like this in 30 years. He was a steady sipper, not a chugger. That was one of the few things he had truly learned in college. He couldn't successfully chug beer and expect to remain in control of his emotions or stomach content. And he'd already drunk at least half a fifth of Jack. That was bad news. Skip shook his head when the usher indicated it was time for him to stroll up to the coffin to deposit his tabs. He didn't have any anyway. He ~~that~~ thought the whole scheme was an urban legend and he never could figure out why Buddy would want to collect pop tabs, what he did with them, or where they all went. All the collections did was give false hope to the stupid and the sick. Skip knew Marty felt exactly as he did and wondered what he had up his sleeve, both of which were fluttering like high-seas pirate sleeves in the wind. The guy had to be freezing. Without the thermal whiskey, surely he would have been, Skip thought.

Ka-plushhh!!! Number four. He was no longer chugging so much as chewing. He was full up at the throat and had to fight to get it down. Skip suspected the suds was fighting to free themselves, too. He had so much unspent carbonation in him, Skip was surprised he wasn't floating above the tombstones. He didn't like where this was heading but there was nothing he could do to intervene. His feet felt like he was wearing 100-pound concrete stompers on both feet.

Ka-plushhh!!! He couldn't have been draining it any faster if he'd been pouring it right onto the ground. Part of Skip wanted to stop him, hustle him off into the woods where he could be sick. But another part was fascinated by what might happen. It was terrifying and exhilarating. But given the beer and whiskey consumption, he felt sure it was going to be messy.

Ka-plushhh!!! A six-pack in under 15 minutes. It was a damn-the-torpedoes performance that would have been remembered by all who saw it. But it wasn't the beer consumption they'd most remember. What happened next was.

Marty tore the top off the sixth beer can and looked down at the little metal tabs jingling in his palm. Tears were running down his face and no one could tell whether they were from grief or alcohol. It didn't matter. He staggered to the end of the line and lurched back and forth as the five in front of him ploddingly shuffled forward to pour their pop tabs into the container, which must have weighed 50 pounds by now. If measured in minutes it would have been enough time to prolong the life of an ailing child for about 16 months. A precious gift.

Grieving people allow other grievers their space. No behavior is too odd at a funeral among mostly strangers. So no one seemed to mind underdressed Marty getting smashingly gassed within feet of the coffin during the middle of a Minnesota winter. No one seemed to mind that he was going to take six fresh pop tabs and drop them into the large hamper. In a way, it seemed oddly touching — as long as he didn't vomit in the hamper, the hole or anywhere within eyeshot of tombstones. That would have been just sick.

When it came his turn at the container, everyone was on their feet watching to see what would happen. He stood before the container at the head of Buddy's final container and seemed to sway like a scarecrow suspended on a weather-warped cross. He tilted back so far that a couple of mourners in the front row stepped forward like mosh pit do-gooders ready to catch a body surfer headed for the concrete. But, amazingly, his internal gyroscope somehow righted the lurch in time. With both hands he caught the edges of the container and Skip was sure he was going to heave into the big tab tub.

But he didn't. Instead, he turned to address the crowd. A thin fireman's pole of drool drizzling out one corner of his mouth to the lapel of his jacket where the subfreezing temperatures were quickly turning it into ice art. Marty was smiling when he looked up. It was a suicide so everyone was hoping for a CSI-type revelation, but they were disappointed. Sort of.

"I never had a laugh without wishing Buddy would be there to share it with me. He had a sleepless curiosity and a love for his fellow man — even the worst of us — that was unmatched."

He waved a hand grandly to his side. "You need look no farther than this pile of little metal miracles to know that. He was always thinking of others."

He closed his eyes and didn't speak for so long everyone thought he'd passed out on his feet. That's what Skip thought, and he almost moved forward to put a steadying arm around his friend when Marty jolted upright.

"Up until the end," Marty said with an acid hiss. "He wasn't thinking of us when he put that gun to his head, was he?"

Mitch Kimble shifted uncomfortable as his grandson Sean, suddenly alive with interest, looked up at his grandfather.

"He couldn't have been thinking of us when he pulled that trigger, could he? No. How in God's name could he? That's what we all want to know, isn't it? Why? We all know about his philanthropic work here and we all certainly support it. We pull our little tabs off our beers and sodas and tuck them into little jars so we can help the sick kids get better. It's so, so, soooo beautiful."

By now he was so, so, soooo drunk, his sarcasm was sounding sincere. Skip made a bet with himself that he'd be vomiting on the coffin in three minutes. He checked his watch.

"But I'm not like Buddy. I don't care about those strangers, those poor sick kids. I care about Buddy. The kids can go to hell for all I care."

This sent a buzz of alarm through the crowd. Wishing sick kids to hell was really sick, and not the kind of sick that could be fixed with a dump truck full of pop tabs. It was a mangy dog kind of sick somebody should put out of its misery.

"He believed there was magic in these pop tabs," he slurred. "While I do not, I do believe in Buddy. That's why I bought these magic beers. I don't want minutes for Buddy's Buddies. I want minutes from Buddy. I want to ask him one question. Why? I figure six minutes is enough time to get a sound answer."

It had been a busy couple of days down at Klipstein LaPlant & Sons the night the coroner brought Buddy's body in. Mrs. Jackson had died in her sleep down at the nursing home. She'd been sick for a long time and they wanted to get her pallid skin a pretty shade of pink that would please her kin. Poor Henry Barker had died when a milk truck skidded across the ice down near the Twin Cities and mangled his 62-year-old body so badly he bled to death before the paramedics could get there. His face, however, was fine and Kurt and Ralph just put some stuffing in his best suit, shined his shoes, and he was good to go. Mr. and Mrs. Weyerd died of carbon monoxide poisoning after he forgot to shut the running car off in the garage, the poor dears. Their youngest daughter had just left for her last semester at college and they were planning their first trip out west since the kids left the nest.

People were dying in droves. Business was booming.

But they didn't have any time to pretty up Buddy's body. It would certainly be a closed casket funeral anyway. For Pete's sake, the guy blew half his head off. Who'd want to see that? So they drained him of his once vital bodily fluids and stitched the hole shut and filled him with some chemicals that would preserve the body in the event they could, well, maybe regenerate him some day. That's just what they did.

When Marty lifted the coffin lid to scatter his six pop tabs across his chest, revulsion froze all the mourners.

"Well, why'd you do it, Buddy?" Marty asked with a conversational tone. "I paid my dues there. You owe me six minutes and one answer. Why? We'd have helped you. Anyone of us. If it was something that couldn't be fixed, just raise a finger. Say something. Or wink that one eye."

It seemed later to Skip that Marty had somehow transferred all his drunkenness to the rest of the room and

Marty was the sober one, the only one who could act with clarity and decisiveness. It made for quite a show.

"What? Six minutes not enough? Here, take some more." He reached both hands deep into the bin and brought up two huge fistful of pop tabs and sprinkled them across the lap and stomach of his dead friend. "That ought to do it. C'mon, man, I've given you a hundred precious minutes there. Answer me."

Skip distractedly figured Marty had about 60 seconds before he heaved his stomach up into the coffin and made a scene.

"Playing hard to get, eh?"

And this was when it became a real spectacle, something everyone would remember and recount for years to come. It was horrifying, but every one was glad they were there, because Marty gave them all a really great story.

Marty somehow summoned the stability and the strength to turn and lift the entire 50-pound bin of pop tabs and pour the entire contents into the coffin. He thought that'd be enough to bring him back to life and maybe do the Lazarus Macarena for joyous guests. But it wasn't. Buddy was deader than hell.

LaPlant reacted first. As the silver waterfall cascaded into the coffin, he raced from the back and jumped at Marty like a charging linebacker. But Marty was ready for him. He staggered the onrushing funeral director with a sharp elbow to the solar plexus. LaPlant stumbled against the latch holding the middle strap tight and knocked it free. Two, still, would have been enough to secure the coffin, he figured later. But not with 50 pounds of metal pop tabs that Marty had poured in. And even if — if — the two straps could have handled that 240 or so pounds, there was no way they could have handled the additional 175 pounds of living, breathing, corn puking, off-balance Marty McCrae that went spilling into the coffin after he'd thrown the elbow at LaPlant.

It teetered there for three full seconds, just long enough for everyone to produce an indelible mental snapshot before the whole works went crashing six feet into the frozen ground with a force that slammed the lid shut on Marty and Buddy in one last Buddy-buddy embrace.

After that, the mourners rushed out like they were late for a cleansing shower after a swim through a toxic swamp. Sean thought it was the coolest thing he'd ever seen. As an adult he wrote a minor best selling novel based on the comedic commotion.

The two gravediggers spent an hour extricating the nearly comatose McCrae from the stinking coffin. They spent the night telling interested strippers about the whole thing and for the first time felt rather proud to be involved in such an exciting occupation.

They left all the pop tabs in the coffin with Buddy, and that's what was most upsetting to all those who attended. The children would never get those minutes collected from Buddy's funeral. Gone forever. Left to molder in the ground, of no good to no one. It was really such a sad, sad waste.

Of course, Marty thought, the same could have been about Buddy.

DECEMBER 2080

The voluptuous little wind chime of a girl had breezed in again for what Marty figured was the 10th time in the past two weeks. Even her shapely shadow was prettier than many of her envious flesh and blood contemporaries. She was about five-foot-two, fair skin, rust red hair and lively green eyes that danced like ballerinas around the room whenever she talked about the man she said was her late grandfather.

"I want to know everything you can tell me about him," said Orla O'Malley. "I want to know what made him laugh, what made him sad, if he liked puppies, where he liked to relax, where —"

"— he hid all his money?"

She gave Marty a lopsided frown that was half scold, half smile. She'd told Marty she was the seventh grandchild of Will Ponce's seventh daughter. Marty heard that and immediately began calling Orla O'Malley "Double-Oh Seven." Marty had seen other secret agents come in on treasure hunts before but there was something about this one that seemed authentic or, at least, as Buster deduced, cute enough to engage. Through more than a dozen visits, she'd confided that she was highly invested in her grandfather's

Acme Pharmaceuticals. He guessed she was about 20, but she was coy about her age.

"Really, I'm just trying to find out more about him," she said. "You guys were best friends, no?"

"Yes, no," said Marty. "Or no, yes. It depends on how we unravel the French-like way you posed your question. Buddy was always my best friend. Even after he'd killed himself. There are times I still prefer spending time with the solitary memory of his company to the company of many actual living human beings. Buddy was the best. Even hungover, he was just excellent to be around. I remember many hungover days when we'd enter a tavern at 1 o'clock and wouldn't leave until 2 o'clock, but — speaking of riddles — we weren't there an hour. It was 13 hours. Entire groups of people would come in, get roaring drunk, and toddle back to their homes while we stayed and made friendly with the bartender. He'd never let a hangover defeat him. I didn't think anything could. Years later, I found out a shotgun to the face did. I'm sure, given another 13 hours in the bar, I could have talked him out of it. Hell, I bet I could have done it in seven."

"Wow," she said. "Thirteen hours of stationary drinking. That is a long time. Wasn't it difficult?"

"I quote Buddy who said when asked the same question, 'The first nine hours were a little rough.'"

"But if Buddy and you were so buddy-buddy, how come all the exhibits in the museum were of you and Grandpa Ponce?"

"Ah, good ol' Grandpa Ponce," Marty said. "I don't mean to diminish our association, but we were more like business partners than best buddies. Certainly not the way

I was buddies with Buddy. Will and I had a blast together, always, but there was always a contentiousness to our friendship. I exerted tremendous effort to try and get him to relax and enjoy life. But he always had one more mountain to climb. After our incarcerations, he sort of appropriated me as a business expense. But, really, I fit better with him in some ways than I did with any of my wives. Wives always wanted me to work and thought it was shameful when I'd want to sit around and philosophize."

Not so with Will, Marty explained. "Will wanted me around because I was an idea guy. And he understood a really good idea guy thinks best when he's relaxed. So he gracefully ensured I'd always have access to liquor, golf, cigars, bourbon and interesting women. Those were rarely permissible when wives were around."

"I remember the big gulf oil spill of 2010," Marty said. "It was one hell of a mess. Nobody could figure out what to do. Me, I was horrified, too. But one day after a round of golf, I was having a plate of delicious blackened salmon. I chose the salmon because I'd just read it was among the healthiest of sea bounty because it was considered an 'oily' fish, and a rich source of omega 3 polyunsaturated fatty acids which help reduce the risks of heart disease. Amazingly, food described with words like polyunsaturated, fatty and acid is actually good for you. Who'd have guessed?

"So while every one else was running around trying to remove the fish from the oil, I figured it would be beneficial to mankind if we could teach the fish to eat and enjoy all the oil that was at the time making many of them extinct. Gulf fish supercharged on pure oil had the potential to be the healthiest fish ever produced. And after some complaints and with some modifications, Will was able to genetically design a fish that saved the gulf by eating the oil. Plus, it made it really handy when you wanted to deep fry a fish. Just throw it on the grill and it deep fries itself from the inside out I even came up with the perfect industry slogan: 'Eat Oil-Enriched Gulf Fish! Crude enough to put in your engine. Refined enough to put on your plate!'"

But, of course, it was in the realm of drugs, where Will made his biggest scores. While the rest of the pharmaceutical world was going nuts trying to make soft things longer and harder, Marty said someone would make a fortune if they made short hard things much less loathsome.

"Understand, I'm talking toenails. It turned the pharmaceutical industry on its, shall we say, head," he said, allowing himself a mirthful little grin. "He came up with the pill that brought all toenail growth to a halt. That saved marriages. You're too young to remember, but men used to hate to cut their own toenails and they'd grow to dangerous lengths. I remember I once severed the Achilles' tendon of one of the Kim wives. I can't remember which one, but she nearly bled to death. I told Will about it from the emergency room and swore that the man or woman who came up with a pill that prevented the halted the growth of toenails would make a fortune. Toenails are not like hair. Only the fetishists want to stroke, kiss or admire a really well-coiffed toe. It doesn't matter if you attend a fancy shindig with them longer or shorter. They just need to be uniform. By the way, you do know that the origin of shindig comes from a prairie party where the dancing was so raucous feet got dug into the shins. I'll wager they weren't too careful about the toenails out on the prairie.

"Anyhoo, Will went right to work coming up with a series of pills that would end the need for toenail clippers forever. He never came up with just one pill. He understood you can't make money selling someone something just once. He knew you needed to addict them so they'd need to come back again and again and again. So millions of people paid $1,200 for 24 monthly treatments of Toehalta nail retarders. It would have worked with one pill and that would have saved a lot of trouble, because after a dozen or so treatments, everything stopped growing. It was fine for older people who'd already stopped growing and were satisfied with the length of their hair.

"But the pill froze for years many young girls at diminutive stages in their development. It wasn't really that bad for your granddaddy because it meant he had to sell them a whole raft of new drugs to jump start the growth of the rest of them."

Just recounting all the legal drugs and their surprising side effects made Marty as dizzy as if he were consuming them.

There were run-amok drugs meant to personalize complexions that altered shades according to barometric pressures. There were anti-depressant pills that left users in such a euphoric state they had to simultaneously pop prescribed depressants to keep the rampant giddiness at bay. When users of popular diabetes drug began to report the loss of their fingerprints, criminals began taking a drug whose warning label said side effects may include diabetes.

There were drugs to make homely people appear prettier, ones that made talkative people restrict their verbosity, drugs that made people work faster, sleep more deeply and have erections that lasted longer than three hours when, by God, everyone realized sleepless woodies were what everyone craved. The people soon demanded a pill that offered four-hour erections as its main purpose and not an unintended side effect.

And all the while, Will was using his massive profits to research the one drug that would have the biggest impact on world since the crucified Christ rolled aside the rock and went for an Easter stroll.

Will was after a pill that would let people live forever.

"If he could make and patent that pill, he could keep selling it to people over and over and over," Marty said. "It became his obsession."

Orla, as she always did, leaned forward when he mentioned, as he always did, Ponce's quest for the Holy Grail of drugs — the one that would lead to an eternal need for more and more drugs. It was Ponce's obsession.

"Do you have any idea how far along he was in his experiments?" she said.

"No, I never cared about any of that stuff."

"Did he ever talk to you about his plans?"

"Yes, often," Marty said. "But I'd tell him to stop tampering with nature and enjoy his life. He said he wanted to contribute something everlasting to mankind before he quit. I told him if he was serious about that then he should stop making and selling drugs."

"What if someone offered you a drug that would let you live forever? Would you take it?"

"Ha! I feel like I already have lived forever. My body is broken down. I'm all used up. No thanks."

"Isn't there anything anyone could say or do that would make you want to live forever?" Orla asked. "Nothing?"

"Well, there's Jesus, of course," Marty said. "All my life the Born Agains have been loudly assuring me that He's coming back. 'Any day now!' they say. I'd like to meet Jesus and ask him why He and His father have allowed this world to become such a sad, godforsaken mess. I've even wondered if it wasn't the result of excessive prayer."

Marty told her about how in 2041 he proposed a National No-Pray Week to give God a break. He knew for thousands of years people had been praying for better health, for riches, for love and to end the myriad suffering in this big, sad world of woe. That wasn't all. Startled students were always muttering silent prayers for divine recollection during pop quizzes, patients were praying the golf-mad doctor wasn't not too distracted by his afternoon tee time to perform lifesaving surgery, and drunks in bars were praying He would help steer the car to safety and surreptitiously past the DUI road blocks.

And, yes, like beauty contestants, everyone was always praying for world peace. And where had it all gotten us? It seems, once again, to the brink of destruction. People all over the world are being slaughtered, usually in God's name. In nearly every major conflict, God was usually the mutual justification for the holy hell that was erupting around the world.

For God's sake, Marty figured, it was high time to try something new. He proposed a "National No-Pray Week" where America closed the churches and ceased any and all prayers to God Almighty. And, no, that didn't mean substituting any pagan idols.

"My point was, 'Don't stop believing in God. Just quit bugging Him all the time.' Too many people pray every night that God will change the world and then spend the rest of the next day ignoring all the God-given powers each has to change the world."

Marty figured He might enjoy the leisure and reward us by eliminating world hunger or at least giving us a carefree week without extreme weather conditions. It was worth a try. No one could argue that more than 2,000 years of steadfast prayers had made the world a better, more peaceful place. On the contrary, even with all that prayer, it still seemed now more than ever that the whole wicked world is — God help us — going straight to hell. If we didn't try something new, he feared the world didn't have a prayer.

"So, you see," Marty said, "I have a lot of questions for Jesus. I don't want to live forever, and nobody in this endless line wants me to, that's for sure, but I hope I can stick around long enough to see Jesus. He's coming, they say. Well, I'm going. If He's ever going to fulfill my lifelong dream, then He'd better get in here and get in line."

Orla's time was ticking down. "Thanks, Mr. McCrae," she said. "I'll be back soon. I love hearing your stories about my grandfather."

"Please, call me Marty," he said. "Your granddaddy was a puzzle I could never solve. I never could get him to relax. He was the most driven man I ever met. I thought I could help him. I was wrong. And now he's gone, lost in space for 20 years now. He'd probably love this, me being involved in something that's making so much money, even if it wasn't for me."

"Ah, he loves you," she said. "He's always looked up to you. He was just telling me how your gift was an ability to enrich lives one conversation at a time. It still amazes him."

Her smile was hot cocoa after a long walk in the snow. It was so charming, Marty temporarily forgot his confusion that he thought he heard her refer to her grandfather in the present tense. Before he could recover to ask her about the apparent slip — *wheeeee!!!* — she was gone, instantly replaced by a near destitute gambler who'd taken out a $10,000 loan on the fraudulent pretense that the money would be used for home repairs. He'd be fleeing the country in six months.

Marty figured he'd quiz Agent 007 about her grammatical slip up when he saw her in the next day or so. But she didn't show up the next day or the day after that. In fact, she never showed up in the three intervening months between her apparent slip and the onset of McCrae's coma.

By then he'd forgotten all about it anyway.

MARCH 2081

He must have heard what seemed to him to be about 300 people who misused the word "humbug" over what he thought was going to be his last Christmas. Careless language always infuriated him the way flag mistreatment infuriates patriots.

He adored humbug and wanted to unshackle it from its Christmas prison. That's why he teased people with it clear into March.

"Do you remember the band, U2?" he asked Victor Crenshaw, a 74-year-old retired optician from Salinas, California.

"Why, yes, I do," Crenshaw said.

"Very good! Then perhaps you remember how singer Bono introduces the song, 'Helter Skelter,' on their album 'Rattle and Hum,'" he said. "He says, 'This is a song Charles Manson stole from the Beatles. We're stealing it back.' Well, in 1843 Charles Dickens stole the word 'humbug' from proper usage. Now, I'm stealing it back."

McCrae maintained that humbug had to do more with WMD, Ponzi schemes, crooked politicians and reality TV than any dyspeptic dislike for Christmas. True American humbug, he said, raged all year long.

"Buster, toss me that dictionary, will you?" Buster tossed it to Marty without bothering to look up. Marty at times thought he was breaking through, but mostly Buster never did anything that would convince any old alien he wasn't anything more than a flaming orifice. Marty thumbed to page 343 of the dog-eared American Heritage Dictionary he'd received in high school. It had survived every technological advance that had sought to make it obsolete.

"See here, Victor, it defines humbug as: '1. A hoax, fake; 2. an impostor or charlatan; 3. Nonsense, rubbish.' Of course, our dictionaries are compiled by — and I'm making what may be a wild and unfair assumption here — pointy-headed dorks whose cloistered existences allow no popular culture references to illuminate the inner walls of their ivory towers. And pop culture is from whence the power of the humbug misusage stems."

Crenshaw by now had the look of a chicken in the rain. His wife had given him $50 and the afternoon to visit the museum and take a chance that McCrae would expire. He was right now wishing he'd spent the $50 on a burger and a beer at Keen's Steakhouse. McCrae was really off and running. He looked over at Buster and wondered how he wasn't brain dead from the repetitiveness of the monologues.

"'Bah Humbug' is the pejorative phrase most associated with our most powerful story of Christmas redemption,' he said. "It first appears on the third page of 'A Christmas Carol,' and I just happen to have a copy of it right here.

He said this as if he expected Crenshaw to squeal with girlish delight. Crenshaw looked at the clock and saw there were still 9 minutes and 30 seconds left and felt the first pangs of low grade claustrophobia gnawing at his stomach.

"Ah, here it is: 'A merry Christmas, Uncle! God save you!' cried a cheerful voice. It was the voice of Scrooge's nephew, who came upon him so quickly that this was the first intimation he had of his approach.

Now, note here as I provide the punctuation: 'Bah (exclamation point),' said Scrooge. 'Humbug (exclamation point).

"'He had so heated himself with rapid walking in the fog and frost, this nephew of Scrooge's, that he was all in a glow; his face was ruddy and handsome; his eyes sparkled, and his breath smoked again.

"'Christmas, a humbug, Uncle!' said Scrooge's nephew. 'You don't mean that, I am sure?'

"'I do,' said Scrooge. 'Merry Christmas! What right have you to be merry? What reason have you to be merry? You're poor enough.'

"'Come, then,' returned the nephew gaily. 'What right have you to be dismal? What reason have you to be morose? You're rich enough.'

"'Scrooge, having no better answer ready on the spur of the moment said, 'Bah! again; and followed it up with 'Humbug.'"

"See there!" Marty exulted. "Clearly, he's referring in two distinct declarations that the idea of a happy holiday is an excessive hoax or fraud. As the book progresses, each subsequent reference to humbuggery refers, not to seasonal Christmas elements, but to something that might be cooked up by the likes of a crafty magician.

"When apparitions of old Marley's head replace those of Biblical figures depicted on artistic fire place tiles, Scrooge exclaims, 'Humbug!' Inexplicable banging from down the stairs? 'It's humbug still! I won't believe it.' As Marley's ghost begins to diminish into the ether, Dickens writes, 'He tried to say 'Humbug!' but stopped at the first syllable.'"

The old devotee of humbuggery told Crenshaw as he did countless others that the word appears in its proper form in "The Wizard of Oz."

"Certainly, a white-haired old grandpa like you caught that one, didn't you?" he asked. "The Scarecrow is so incensed that the Wizard is a fraud that he stammers until he comes up with the most devastating word he can find to describe him in those days when profanity was kept off the silver screens and reserved for places like loading docks. The Wizard admits he's not a wizard at all and the Scarecrow says, 'You … you … you humbug!' Watch for it. It happens right after Toto pulls the curtain back. And, not to get off track, but did you know that Toto is played by a dog that was really named Toto? Makes you wonder if it was coincidence or just really expert casting. Still, nothing Christmasy about Oz and the Emerald City."

There were still four minutes left when McCrae told Buster to ask Dudash to bring him a bowl of Lucky Charms. It was there in forty seconds. He took a silver spoon so sizable it made McCrae look like a little kid in the spacious Hygiene Comfort Clean 2500. He stopped talking and began to prospect among the cereal so he'd have nothing left but the marshmallows. Crenshaw thought he was off the hook when McCrae startled him with another outburst in defense of humbuggery.

"In fact, the misappropriation of the humbug must be infuriating to an egotistical Dickens contemporary who so reveled in the joy of artful humbug that he in his 1855 autobiography called himself "The Prince of the Humbugs.""

"That would be P.T. Barnum. The satirical fingerprints of America's most authentic impresario are all over America even today and are thriving right here in this room. Want some pure humbug, American-style? Barnum enjoyed his first commercial success in 1835 by purchasing for $1,000 an elderly slave woman named Joice Heth, who he claimed to be the 161-year-old nurse to George Washington. Paying audiences sat in rapt attention as the blind, toothless and withered ancient spun religious and patriotic tales about being the de facto mother to the father of the country. Days after her February 1836 demise, Barnum allowed newspaper skeptics to autopsy her brittle remains. Hired medical examiners cried fraud and said, humbug, she wasn't a day over 80. Barnum then fueled the uproar by declaring the autopsy was a fake and that the real Heth, now pushing 162 years old, was alive and well — and still drawing huge crowds — in Connecticut.

"He then had the audacity to offer a third 'real' story: that he'd found Heth in Kentucky, yanked all her teeth, taught her baby General Washington anecdotes and that he'd capriciously increased her age by 10 years along the tour until she'd finally hit 161.

"It was humbug upon humbug! The story made a real impression on me. And I hope I've made one on you, my friend."

He didn't wait for Crenshaw to answer.

"The point of all this that you and I are besieged by humbug and the moralists decry that the decay is eating away at the soul of America's character. To that, I say, 'Bah! Uh, hogwash!' Roll with the punches, Victor! Roll with the punches, America! The hyperbole is a uniquely American phenomenon. Sit back and savor all the silliness."

His timing was by now honed to perfection. There were just four seconds left when he addressed the slack-jawed Crenshaw with a warm closing salutation: "And may you enjoy a warm and Happy Humbug today and and all year long!"

Then — *wheeeee!* — like that he was gone. Crenshaw'd said maybe five words for the entirety of his 14 minute, 59 second visit. He was immediately replaced by a no-nonsense Girl Scout from Jakarta who was eager to earn her Gold Star Achievement Award. Neither Crenshaw nor the Girl Scout had any way of knowing that in eight minutes McCrae would be as good as dead, stricken by a coma, and that both of them would be highly sought interviews.

What had begun with so many joyful expectations would descend into a pit of despair from which no one would no emerge untainted by the unseemliness of it all as the last baby boomer clung to life's twilight.

Commentators called it a legal quagmire, a human tragedy and an unsavory farce.

None thought to headline it a humbug.

IN DREAMVILLE …

Besides introductions and asides, Buddy'd been mostly silent throughout his visits to Dreamville. Now he took over a sort of multi-media presentation the kind he used to uniformly sleep through back when he and Marty were in college.

Marty poured himself a big glass of bourbon and settled back into the big blue breast chair to enjoy the show.

On the screens flashed a picture of the 103-year-old Marty and Marty flattered himself by thinking, hey, I sure looked young back then. The picture was captioned "New Year's Day 2067. Marty remembered resolving on that day to prepare for his death by sequestering himself in his New York apartment and awaiting the Apocalypse. Evidence that it was coming was mounting daily and Marty wanted to be sure he didn't miss a minute of it. By then, the only thing preferable to the end of the entire world would have been the end of his meager, singular contributions to it.

"Now, correct me if I'm wrong," Buddy said, half-smiling, "But for the previous 12 or so years you'd go to sleep every evening praying that Jesus would call you home, right? But the Lord was either not calling or had lost your number. You'd been moving around so much that you were probably pretty hard to find without the benefit of some alien butt chip. You moved into this 57th Street brownstone," — the picture changed — "with every intention that it would be your last address. You were 89 and figured you'd never live to see 90. You'd already bested the actuarial tables by twelve years. You'd buried all your dogs, all your friends, the last being Skip and his death had left ~~him~~ *you* thoroughly depressed."

What Buddy'd said had been true. It had been a very melancholy time for Marty. Skip's last years had been a cruel torture. Diabetes had claimed first his left foot just below the knee. Then after 16 months of testing and failed treatments, his right was hacked off. Born with four working limbs, Skip was entombed with just one. A boy whose parents named him Skip after his father's old World War II Navy buddy spent the last five years of his life confined to a wheelchair in an old folks home furiously insisting everyone ought to call him Rollie. Marty said a prayer that his old friend was somewhere crowded with horny, naked, harp-strumming supermodels. He thought his cranky old friend deserved a break. He wanted to ask Buddy if he knew, but somebody'd depressed the mute button controlling his voice. He was speechless.

"Your ties to the earthly world were one-by-one disappearing. All your lovers were gone. The children you'd sired knew of you not. The life that had been so rich, so full of laughter and mirth, had finally grown tedious. You'd done it all and there was nothing left to do but die, and death you did not fear."

He didn't fear death, but he was terrified of how he was going to die and the many awful ways it might happen. As Buddy ticked them off, flashes of mayhem flooded the screens. He remembered not wanting to burn up in a fire, get run down by a bus, drown in a flood or have a building fall on him in an earthquake. He didn't want his frail frame to be swept away in a tornado, and he would have hated to be in a doomed sub at the bottom of the ocean saying quiet, earnest prayers as the remaining breaths ticked away in fetid silence. He didn't want to be in a car wreck where he survived, but was trapped and invisible at the bottom of a deep gorge, his dying screams reckoned only by squirrels, raccoons and the occasional passing Sasquatch. He didn't want to die of malpractice at the hands of some fumble-fingered surgeon who didn't remember where he'd left that pesky scalpel.

Dying of cancer would have been unpleasant, for sure, but he remembered hearing as a child that each cigarette scissored seven minutes off each life, and that made him feel rather hopeful and in control of his demise.

"So you began smoking Camel unfiltered cigarettes like a fiend," Buddy said and the crowd roared. The story of his life was entertaining even the strangers, he reckoned.

Buddy told how Marty'd gotten rid of all his household computers when some particularly nasty hackers began disseminating computer viruses that infected the human users with honest-to-goodness venereal diseases. All the viral e-mails were slugged "ILOVEYOU," and word got around pretty quick that opening attachments to these e-mails would give you a nasty dose of the clap. But people were so desperate for affection they couldn't help themselves. They opened up the e-mails to find out who virtually loved them and wound up getting much the same fate scores of misled lovers had earned the old-fashioned way.

"It made you nostalgic for the good old days when computer viruses merely wiped out hard drives, not hard-ons," Buddy said and everyone laughed. "You figured your last Earthly conversation before forever retreating to the comforting glow of your television was with an angry agnostic who maintained religion was the opiate of the people. You argued it was television."

The screen filled with a simulated version of the actual day with hammy over-actors playing Marty and the agnostic.

"'Question with boldness even the existence of God; because if there is one, he must more approve of the homage to reason than that of blindfolded fear,' that was Thomas Jefferson," the acting agnostic said with haughty precision. "That's why I'm an agnostic. My fealty is to reason. Religion is for fools."

"You're getting off the subject," said the man playing Marty, who thought the actor was too stuffy to play him. "I'm not here to argue agnosticism with you. I'm saying television is the opiate of the people. If Door No. 1 is heaven and Door No. 2 is television, the contestants will all opt for Door No. 2. Heaven's too hard to comprehend, but everyone's hip to, say, 'Green Acres.' 'You can't go wrong with Door No. 2 — or can you?' That's what Monte Hall said."

"Who's Monte Hall?"

"Never mind."

Buddy began talking over a montage that showed each actor going about their days as the events played out. "You both walked away selfishly satisfied each had won the argument. The agnostic went on-line to a chat room to boast of his superior sophistry and wound up with a nasty dose of clap after foolishly opening an "ILOVEYOU" e-mail he mistakenly thought would be an admiring epistle. You went home, sparked a cigarette and enjoyed a particularly funny episode of "Green Acres."

"Still, for pure humor, you never missed the news. The works of the social engineers well-meaning ways were beginning to bear fruit. Their sincere belief that they could manufacture a perfect world was being revealed to be hubris.

"It began innocently enough with itch-illuminator pills. Our friend Will Ponce deemed searching for an itch too inconvenient and invented a pill that caused itches to give off a bluish glow right through clothing so the itch target could be more efficiently identified so helpful friends could scratch them out. He thought it was the next logical step in social networking. That way strangers could helpfully groom one another the way monkeys at the zoo do. He thought it would be a perfect ice breaker. The problem was everyone who took them started giving off soft embarrassing blue glows from seasonal crotch rot."

A picture of a platform full of subway riders with blue glows on their crotches provoked howls of laughter. Marty laughed, too.

"Then things only got worse, culminating in the well-intentioned mistake to clone grandpa," he said. "Remember, Marty? You thought that one was going to kill you, too. The resulting bloodshed from that little stunt made everyone sick and thoughtful enough to reconsider all the scientific advances. It started in the late 1990s when wacky scientists convinced a gullible public that they'd cloned sheep. They paraded two gentle sheep in front of the media and told everyone they'd been cloned from the same cell. Of course, if anyone had been at all observant, they would have realized that there is not one sheep on the planet that doesn't look exactly like every other sheep. In fact, most every sheep on the planet was indistinguishable to everyone but the other sheep, who, if they'd have been hip to the taunt, would have resented the bigoted old line, 'Oh, they all look alike.'"

That got another big laugh.

By then the genie was out of the bottle, Buddy said, and scientists did, indeed, begin cloning cows. Then dogs. Then fish. Then monkeys. No one bothered to clone cats because cats were such numbskulled ingrates. And no one bothered to clone children because children are special, unique and are going to be around a long, long time and, geez, why would anyone want to have kids without the benefit of a really good boink?

But grandparents, that was another matter, Buddy said. When grandparents started aging and edging toward death's door, well-meaning loved ones said, "We don't want our children growing up without the love and warmth of their grandpap. We want him cloned. Just clone the one we got and then maybe give us a spare. Just in case. Same with grandma."

"That was a big mistake. A whopper. A mistake of huge, bloody proportions. While the cloned grandmas mostly stayed home and became expert at things like Eucre, the male clones or the originals — no one could really tell which was which — quickly abandoned the well-meaning families and organized into a huge, out-of-control voting bloc. They were the angry white-haired males."

Marty recalled it all in vivid detail. Prescient politicians began to pander to the angry white-haired males and soon a world that was teetering on the edge of madness took the plunge. Traffic became unbearable with thousands of tiny white heads peeking over the steering wheels from underneath their ball caps, all of them oblivious to the blink, blink, blinking of their inadvertently applied turn signals. Episodes of road rage reached epidemic proportions.

The screens showed a cavalcade of crisis storming across America. A sequence of shots showed violent demonstrations at offices and apartment buildings that had become uninhabitable after the angry white-haired males took over and ordered all the thermostats set at 84 degrees. Countering those pictures were shots of angry white-haired males smugly parading around in nipple-high polyester pants under mismatched garish sweaters over golf logo shirts.

The scene shifted to restaurants around the country being forced to close their doors after armies of angry early birders kept showing up at 4:20 p.m. to shout at the unprepared staffs, complain about the prices, portion sizes and that, hell, no, they had not ordered the Salisbury steak.

"Bring me the liver and onions!"

"You were justifiably sickened, Marty, when the hit squads finally came to round up the cloned grandpas," Buddy said. "That some of the original grandpas were culled with the rest of the herd was unavoidable, but it really proved how out-of-control the world had become. No one ever thought about where their desires and good intentions would lead. Life expectancy was going up, up, up, but no one paused to think if life was worth living after a point. A movie or a book, even the best of either, can't be any good if it goes on forever. In fact, a good ending is better than endlessness. At least for those of you back there on Earth."

Marty was feeling queasy. He liked violence in cartoons, but loathed it in real life. He was so non-violent he was reluctant to tell a joke with a really strong punchline. He was such a reflexive pacifist the only thing he'd ever killed was time. But he was forever confronted with life's unavoidable ugliness. Violence raged around the globe. There was so much of it. And he knew Buddy was right. Even as he knew he'd wake up and be back in Hygiene Comfort Clean 2500 in the coma that wasn't really a coma.

He was exhibit A that no one thought about endings anymore. They thought only of prolongings, extendings and stretchings. No one reasoned that every body was living way too long as it was.

"Nobody, but you my friend, Marty," Buddy said. "Day-by-day, obituary-by-obituary, you were on the march to become the world's oldest man. You sensed it and were furious with your fate. You dreamed of a dreaded day when you were the oldest man on the planet and all the television cameras would crowd around you and the birthday cake with enough candle power to warn large ocean tankers away from rocky shores. You'd seen it a thousand times."

The screens flashed with another preposterous scene of over-the-top actors really laying it on. A honey blond news reporter leaned in and asked a token old-looking man, "And do you have anything you want to tell the viewers?"

The poor tortured soul mumbled something into the ear of the blonde newscaster and she leaned in and she'd translate, "He says he owes it all to clean living!" when

Marty and any sensible senior new what he really said was, "Yes, please, someone kill me!"

The crowd seemed to relish the simulations the best. This one got the biggest laugh of all.

"By the time it was 2068, the men and women Will Ponce left behind cured most cancers, heart disease, diabetes, HIV, Alzheimer's, flesh-eating bacteria and simple chronic halitosis," Buddy said. "It was becoming impossible for seniors to die of natural causes. That meant violence was the only solution. The old timers had become much like house flies, and you never see a house fly simply fall out of the sky stricken with a heart attack. No. The only way flies die is violently. They'd get their guts smeared on the walls when someone cranked up a rolled-up newspaper and on the fifth try finally made contact. Splat!"

And that's what started happening with seniors just like him, Marty remembered.

"As the killer diseases began to disappear, death needed to find other ways to meet its dark quota. Bored octogenarians were getting struck by buses by the score," Buddy said. "They lived riskier lives in the hopes they'd finally die. Skydiving accidents where the parachutes mysteriously did not deploy became less and less newsworthy as the skies rained senior citizens. Splat! Suicide by indifference.

He felt a chill as he saw Buddy turn to his right revealing a rotting gunshot wound in his temple. Trick of the light, Marty thought.

It wasn't dying that terrified, Marty. It was how he was going to die. He thought about taking a tombstone tour of all his dead friends around the country, but was afraid some vigilante group would mistake him for an angry white-haired male and gun him down right there in the cemetery. Not the way he wanted to go. He wanted to die in his sleep and prayed every night he wouldn't wake up the next morning. So, instead, he threw the windows in his tiny apartment open during the day and got rid of all the fly swatters. In the summer his apartment became a small buzzing sanctuary. The neighbors all thought he was nuts.

"But waiting to die gets mighty boring, even with the opiate of television," Buddy said. "So, finally, you resolved on New Year's Day 2078 to ignore every resolution you'd ever remembered making. You began using your natural right hand with abandon. You began blistering innocent ears with X-rated profanity during inappropriate conversations. And you began venturing out of your apartment to weekly dance lessons. You'd always wanted to be a dancer. Who knew? And you began daily trips to the park to fatten up already plump pigeons while pondering their apparent indestructibility.

"Then you met Buster and everything changed."

SEPTEMBER 25, 2083

He woke up smiling. If his precise calculations were correct, Martin J. McCrae was doomed to die today. Marshall Palley III was no longer Marshal Marshall Palley. He'd quit marshalling the day after McCrae fell into his coma. That's how confident he was that that undetectable toxins were working. His smugness over the plan had become all encompassing. He'd foiled the best detection systems in the world and had been leaching toxins through dispersant devices lodged in the soles of his shoes. Exposure in small doses was proving harmless to normal adults but was, he hoped, fatal to those 118 years old.

Really, it wouldn't have taken much.

Illicit drugs had been at the heart of the Poncey Scheme that robbed him of his family fortune and and illicit drugs were going to be there when another one came crashing down on the flat, square head of another generation of Palleys, once he got around to finding a suitable mate.

He'd slept in today for the first time in his adult life. He made himself a pot of coffee, read the morning news and once more looked over what he was calling his acceptance speech. It was what he was going to say when the reporters began to swarm. He'd gush about how shocking it was, how much he was going to devote to worthy causes and how $6,250 he'd spent on tickets had been a wise investment. The words like "vendetta," "revenge," "feud" and "blood oath" would not be spoken.

While shaving with the same straight razor that his father and his father before him had used, he practiced looking surprised and overwhelmed in the mirror. The apartment he'd leased and maintained for the past five years was a virtual museum to Palley family heritage. He felt he'd been deigned by fate to correct an historic mistake.

Then he showered and walked down the block to get the fringe chopped off his crew cut. He stopped at the dry cleaners to pick up his snazziest gray suit.

It was going to be a very good day and he'd need to look his best.

⌒﹏﹏⌒

George Prince hadn't even planned on being in New York that day. But the wife of a high-value client had discovered that her spouse was cheating on her with his shapely secretary. She'd hired a burly moving crew and together they ransacked the apartment of the valuables including all George Prince's most artistic pieces. He needed Prince to come and testify to the value of the artistry in a hastily arranged deposition.

Attending at the last minute meant Prince would miss his weekly golf match and the monthly jam session at The Station Inn where he enjoyed performing rag tag bluegrass with doctors, investment bankers, truckers and other successful men and women who uniformly wished they'd made music their life.

The client understood the inconvenience and assured Prince he'd be handsomely compensated. Prince was simple, but he wasn't stupid. He accepted and was soon boarding a first class flight from Nashville to LaGuardia. He was torn about seeing Becky again. He'd tried to put that behind him. He loved her, but with the McCrae carnival now entering in its fifth year, it seemed pointless.

He was convinced the old man — and Prince had grown genuinely fond of him — was never going to die. It was something he couldn't explain. And the whole thing sickened Prince. He had no interest in further participating. Sure, he had fallen for Becky Dudash, but seeing her under these circumstances was an affront to decency he'd nurtured his whole life. Still, he felt an alien itch deep inside him that had nothing to do with surreptitiously embedded monitoring chips.

If he was meant to go, fate would leave him a sign, he told himself.

Still, he was stunned by the sign's bluntness. He figured fate must have figured he was a bit of a bonehead because as he was about to get into a cab following the tedious deposition something shiny caught his eye. He stooped to retrieve it. It was a 1981 coin minted to memorialize Susan B. Anthony. He picked it up and remembered it was the only non-round coin ever minted by the U.S. Treasury Department. In fact, the coin has 11 edges.

And just two sides. A head's and a tail's.

Still not quite believing his eyes, he called heads.

And he gave the old abolitionist suffragette a flip.

Orla O'Malley had for the past four years been waking up every day at 5:30 a.m. But today she'd set the alarm for 7 a.m. and slugged the snooze button for an extra 20 minutes of dozing. She'd need to be rested.

On the walls of the room she used as a de facto lab at her spacious mid-town apartment were chemical engineering degrees from four of the world's most prestigious universities. She showered, toweled off and took a moment, as she always did, to look in the full length mirror on the door where she hanged her towels.

Amazed as always by what she'd been seeing for nearly two years now, she smiled. It was a great way to start every day. She dressed with an endearing jolliness that infused her mornings. But today she wouldn't wear the pert, bright little outfits that favored her figure.

Today's street outfit was more utilitarian and something she could discard in any handy trash can. Beneath it she wore a specially designed form-fitting black jump suit with seven zippered pockets stitched into the sides. She'd loaded the pockets the previous evening. She put on the whole ensemble and was surprised by how comfortable it felt.

She went to the corner diner and ordered country ham eggs benedict that she knew were delicious. She scanned the headlines and saw one of the tabloids had reduced its McCrae coverage to little more than secondary blips. The lack of coverage, of course, hadn't done anything to dampen the draw. On the contrary, the lines snaking through the velvet ropes were longer than ever. Everyone knew McCrae had to die.

Everyone but the girl he called Agent 007 and the secret man for whom she was working.

—⊶✦⊷—

"Send her right in, please," said President Marcia Tender into the Oval Office intercom. She tried to sound composed and restrained. As the door opened, she felt anything but.

"Good morning, Madam President," said Vice President Maggie Cashen. "I understand you wanted to see me."

"Maggie, sit down and, please, let's ditch the silly formalities," she said. "We've been through too much for that any more. Now, I understand you're going to New York again this morning."

It was true. Six years into their second term, Cashen had lost any pretense of caring about the Vice Presidential office. She'd been a key player in the first term, working closely with her old friend Tender. But the steam had gone out of the working relationship, replaced by a tension that evolves between two people whose responsibilities diverge even as their fates intertwine.

Cashen made no secret that she'd become obsessed with the McCrae ghoul pool. If she wasn't in New York waiting in line at the Bolten, she was online reading details. She followed Dudash's blog and often texted her for any scoop she could spill. She'd forsaken all her official duties to follow the minute-by-minute developments from McCrae's suite.

In that regard, she was like 80 percent of the American public.

"Well," Cashen said defensively, "you're so busy running the country I feel like you've completely forgotten about me. You never ask how my day was or what I'm interested in.

With you, it's all treaties this, embargoes that, let's bomb this country, let's negotiate with these guys. We used to be a team and now you walk into the room and I feel like I don't even exist. You won't even look at me. It's humiliating."

Tender stood and removed her glasses. She started in a low voice that sounded like a firehouse siren seconds before the ensuing shriek.

"Do you think it's easy being president?" she said. "I can't fart without the entire free world speculating what I had for lunch. You think I don't wish I could just jump on Air Force One and run up to New York with you and chat with Becky Dudash and get the inside scoop on when she think's Marty McCrae's going to kick? I'd love to do that! Somedays, I dream the two of us could just go and enjoy a jaunt like that. But I can't. Someone has to be the adult in this administration."

At this, Cashen jumped from the sofa and screamed, "And what's that supposed to mean? I've done everything you've asked for the past seven years. I've served you with loyalty and devotion. I think you need to lighten up! You're no fun anymore!"

Historians would debate what happened in the next 15 minutes as a watershed moment in the Tender presidency. All that was known was there was a crescendo of vicious shouting followed by a stillness thorough and alarming enough to warrant the president's chief of staff to dash into the room to investigate.

What he saw would roil the Tender/Cashen administration in unseemly scandal for the remainder of its term.

The president and her vice were locked in a steamy embrace.

━✶━

Nurse Dudash hadn't seen George Prince in eight months. He'd been her toll booth beau, the one she'd fallen for in fifteen minute intervals over the course of four years. He wanted to date her, to move the relationship down the highway. He'd brought her gifts. Things he'd carved. Things he'd found. She had a little treasure chest of items he'd given her as gifts. Love had blossomed, but then her job kept getting in the way. He'd wanted her to take a vacation. She'd not had one in five years. McCrae's dwindling life had consumed hers.

His living was killing her.

She and George had argued. He'd wanted her to take her millions and walk away. She had more than enough and "that much money," he said, "sorta complicates everything."

This little summer gig Dudash had taken to unwind while deciding what to do with the next phase of her life had already "earned" her more than $5 million over the past five years. Throw in the endorsements for nursing uniforms, fingernail polish and under-the-table take from free-spending tabloid muckrakers and she was "worth" about $7 million. She'd already signed a book deal for $1.5 million.

He liked sunsets and sea horses, moonlit walks and the smell of sawdust drifting through his workshop. He liked finding a good parking spot right next to a cheap restaurant that knew how to make a really good cheeseburger. He was a Tennessee cabinet maker who liked simple things.

He would have loved Dudash back in 2078 when she was as delightfully uncomplicated as basic math problems solved with crack calculator apps. Back then she would have gladly run away with him back to Nashville. But now she was stuck. The money was fantastic and it kept rolling in as long as McCrae kept breathing. She was getting rich beyond her wildest dreams.

All because the man down the hall would not die. There was a time when, inexplicably even to herself, she felt she loved Mr. Marty more than any man she'd ever met. He was sweet, understanding, funny, undemanding and had a charm that washed the years off his face every time he smiled. Now, she would have gladly rushed in and pillow-smothered that impassive face until the life finally, blessedly seeped out of him. Two security guards stationed outside the door helped deter any such attack, but she had intimate access. She had the motive and the opportunity. She had everything but the guts. She knew she couldn't do it. Neither could anyone else. Security was ratcheted up with each dialed in bomb, gas, or assassination threat. The penthouse suite at the Bolten Museum housing McCrae was more secure than the Oval Office and what happened at the Bolten mattered more to the country than anything happening at 1600 Pennsylvania Avenue, as the president herself conceded during her July press conference.

Of course, all the conspiracy theorists believed he was already dead, that the coma had been the end of him. That had been 18 months ago and no one back then believed he would have lived out the week. And that was a relief because he'd become a national obsession, one that needed entombment. The obsession had become sickness. The jackpot had become an astronomical obscenity, and the more it grew, the more people began to look at the whole affair as a seamy conceit. But the money was breathtaking. And, geez, the guy had to die someday. Didn't he?

It had been mostly wonderful, right up till the coma 18 months ago. Interesting people, celebrities, politicians, TV weather forecasters — they'd all flirted and fawned over Dudash and Dingus like they were the real celebrities. The effect warped everything about their lives. But the coma changed that. Now, it was as if she and Buster were to blame for McCrae's continuing respiration, a condition that had actually and ironically turned Dudash, a bit role actress, into an actual nurse. She did all the daily maintenance a comatose body required. She cleaned him, exercised him, sponged him and massaged his lifeless muscles, whispered encouragement, and generally tended to him as if he were an expensive Japanese Peace Lilly.

She wanted nothing more than to go to the beach. Any beach. She wanted out of the city, away from the buildings, the crowds, the whispers and the looks. She wanted to spend a month lazing on the sand while the concerns and anxieties of the past six years drained away with the tides. She absentmindedly picked up an unopened bottle of perfume, a gift from Prince. He'd wanted her to wear it on their first date. What the hell? It'd be a shame for it to go to waste, even if she must. She gave herself a short, sweet splash and stood. It was time, again, to tend to her houseplant.

She walked into the room and pointedly ignored Buster, with whom she was barely on grunting terms. She pulled a tray from a shelf in the closet by the bed. She adjusted the waste disposal controls beside the bed. Then, starting at the foot of the bed, she began the exercises that would ward off bedsores, atrophy and the nastiness that comes from being confined to a hospital bed for long stretches at a time. It took about 10 minutes of adjustments as one of the players came and wordlessly went down the chute and another took her place. By the time she'd finished and was leaning over McCrae's serenely silent face as it drew in deep breaths she was shocked to learn the routine and tedium of the past 18 months had ended and she was no longer thinking about being on the beach.

His eyes sprang open and came alive. His ~~his~~ chapped lips parted and he said, "Opium."

It was the first word he'd spoken in 18 months since he'd shouted a profanity at having a hose shoved up his rectum. But "Opium" wasn't a request for painkilling medication. It was the name of the perfume she was wearing. It was shocking, but not as shocking as what caught her eye as she looked over in disbelief at the gape-jawed Dingus.

An erection was pup-tenting the freshly changed sheets.

It was the first of many surprises the day held in store.

What happened next would be litigated in the courts for years. At stake was $989,478,875 and the old ticker was about to run out.

Dingus rushed to the bedside opposite Dudash.

"Did you hear what I heard?" he said. "Did he say 'opium?'"

"Marty, are you awake? Talk to me Marty," she said.

He did more than that. He reached up a bony hand and gave Dudash's face a loving stroke. He pulled it away and she was surprised to see one of her Chardonnay tears had fallen on his finger. She gently removed his hand and held it in hers.

"I was just in the middle of the loveliest dream," McCrae said. "I was in a cheap hotel in York, Pennsylvania, making love to a beautiful women who'd splashed a blast of Opium perfume between her ample breasts and I was frolicking amidst them. What a dream! What a woman!"

"How do you feel?" Dudash asked, a question that was of pressing interest to Martha McGwire. She was a Long Island housewife who was hoping to leave her cheating spouse, Ben, a straying auto body finisher, but really couldn't afford it. Not without $989,478,875, give or take a couple hundred million.

"Why, I am fine. How are you?"

She looked at his clear brown eyes and felt competing surges of anger, joy, and shock cannon ball up and down her spine. He'd been in a coma for the past 18 months and, dammit, didn't look any the worse for wear. She knew this was in defiance of every textbook and soap opera episode she'd studied over the past five years. She'd become a really fine nurse.

"Do you know what day it is?" Dingus asked.

Marty looked at Buster as if he was seeing him for the first time. "My darling little jackass," he sighed. "I haven't known what day it was since 2079."

"You've been in a coma for the past 18 months."

"That's what you think," McCrae said. He was smiling. "I had a seizure, all right, and slipped away toward a bright light. I dreamed I was walking with Jesus. I felt like we were really hitting it off. By God, we were bantering. Then all of a sudden, he smiled at me, shook my hand and gave me a great big shove. I felt myself falling and falling. I landed back in this damned bed in this godforsaken room. I was so morbidly depressed I decided to shut it all down. If I wasn't sleeping I'd just lay there and quietly die. An Indian fakir showed me how. She's probably lived to be 150 years old. She showed me how to shut the human body down like a computer in hibernation and, incidentally, how to enjoy a three hour erection without the benefit of pharmaceuticals. But I decided to power down. Instead of waking up and talking and going through all the motions over and over and over, I just decided to unplug myself, lay here and quietly pray I'd die."

Martha McGwire's prayers were running along those lines, too, as her clock ticked down to five minutes. He'd better get on with it, she thought.

"But, Dudash, your perfume brought back a recollection that was so sweet, I felt a surge of life itself. And I remembered all of a sudden how wonderful life is. This life. Not the next one. Not yet. This is where it's at. This Earth. These people. It was so overwhelming, I just had to express it."

He sat gingerly up in bed and a look of boyish delight creased his face when he saw evidence of an erection down past his waist.

"Why, would you look at that!" he shouted and threw off the covers. "I've got a woodie! An honest-to-goodness hard-on. I haven't even had a soft-on for 30 years! But there it is!" He stared at the erection beneath his pajamas with the beloved wonder new mothers bestow on their babies. Dudash discreetly adjusted the covers to conceal his pride and joy.

"That Opium's powerful stuff, Becky," he said admiringly. "Keep wearing that and you're not going to be single much longer."

The ticker dropped down to zero and — *ding!* — Mrs. McGwire was gone. She'd make her peace with her husband and wound up living happily ever after after all when their 17-year-old daughter came home an unwed mother of a boy she'd named Octavio for reasons she never said. The darling baby became a family adhesive. Ben started coming home straight from work and never again stopped to see Trisha down at the Dilly Dally Deli. They'd found happiness again. All their friends and neighbors, sure that they were bound for divorce, commented on how it was funny how things worked out.

Funny, too, that after Mrs. McGwire disappeared the next person to roll in — the last person to roll in — was George Prince. Becky didn't know if it was the magic of the Opium or the grace of God, but she smiled brightly upon seeing him. She'd really missed him. He smiled back.

Then things got weird. Because in the exact instant before the trap door snapped shut and George Prince could take his place on it, up through the floor popped Will Ponce and Orla O'Malley. They were wearing suction cups strapped to their hands, elbows, and knees. Marty was sure he'd seen a similar get-up on MacGyver.

"Where there's a Will, there's a Way — and here's the Will!" he shouted. "Now, me and my darling granddaughter are here to show you, my old friend, the way!"

They sprang from the hole beaming like mountaineers who'd overcome a particularly difficult peak. Marty blinked away his disbelief to realize that Will didn't look a day older than 38. There were no gray hairs. No worry wrinkles. No gravity ravages. He looked positively pristine, yet he was a mere two years younger than Marty. He looked like he could have been contemporaries with his youthful granddaughter.

Will rushed to Marty's bedside and hugged him with a love that he'd not felt since he was a young man. He didn't know where they'd found a fountain of youth, but he felt like he was feeding off whatever he'd found. His blood felt as if it'd suddenly become carbonated.

Buster sensed it, too, but only in that it meant trouble. Lots of it. He reached in to pull Will off Marty, but Orla was ready for him. She unzipped an inch-long flap over her heart in the black jump suit. From inside, she removed a small aerosol canister and shot a blast right at the back of Buster's neck. The garish ringmaster of *Excesstival!!!* froze like a popsicle.

"See, I told you it would work," Orla said, a triumphant grin on her face.

Dudash stepped out of the way as the grandpa and granddaughter high fived one another. She'd felt herself floating back toward Prince and wasn't at all surprised to realize her hand had drifted snugly into his.

Buster stood exactly as he'd been when the menthol-smelling spray tingled onto his back.

"You haven't killed him, have you ?" Marty said, his voice seeming to betray the fact that such a felony would have been on par with farting at the opera.

"Nah," Will said. "He's fine. In fact, he can see and hear everything we're doing. He just can't move. At least not for the next 10 minutes or so. He's completely immobilized, but he's functioning like a normal human being. Physically, at least. Who knows what he's thinking?"

Orla had taken to studying Buster. Out of courtesy, she angled him toward Marty. She knew he wouldn't want to miss a thing. The left hand that had been gripping Will's jumpsuit was put to his side and its angry grip relaxed. Orla liked the look so much she decided on the spot to raise the right hand in an admiring salute.

Marty chuckled and said, "At ease, my boy, at ease." Buster's eyes were alert and darting back and forth like they were trying to pogo themselves out of his head. "See, that's always been his problem. He's never known how to relax."

He was feeling euphoric, and the atmosphere in the room, for so long so poisonous, felt buoyant. Outside the door, security guards and the endless line of contestants in the world's longest reality show were unaware of the events happening in the suite as the security cameras playing to unwatched monitors on Dudash's unoccupied desk rolled on. Ponce and 007 had spliced in an old tape loop to fool the feed that was broadcasting live around the world.

"It's so good to see you!" he said. "And, George, it's good to see you again."

"Thanks, Marty," Prince said, then turning to Becky, "I can't believe I'm telling you this, but I'm here to ask Becky to marry me. For some reason, I feel like I need your permission."

"Well!" Marty said. "What a day this is turing out to be. First things first. George, Becky, let me introduce you to Will Ponce and his granddaughter Orla O'Malley, who turns out to be more a spy than even I could have guessed. Man, Will, I thought you were dead."

"Not dead, just busy," Will said.

"Busy? You were lost in space!"

"Just because someone's lost doesn't mean they're dead," Orla said. "We didn't really know where we were, but we knew where we were going. We just didn't know how to get there."

"Where were you going?"

"We were on a journey to discover eternal life," Will said.

"Good heavens!" Marty exclaimed. "For God's sake, isn't one life enough?"

"No!" Will cried. "Not when we can live forever. I'm telling you, Marty, things are going to happen here on Earth. Wonderful things. Orla and I spent a good bit of the last six years on Gonto and —"

"Gonto!" Marty said. "You guys know about Gonto?"

It was Orla's turn. "We were looking for a place we could gather all we learned and we tried to find a place where we could apply our minds to higher philosophic study. We wanted to find a place devoid of interesting distractions. And, well, Indiana, was getting rather crowded. Gonto was perfect."

They spent their time there, studying philosophy, eating corn with Jesus and tracking the whereabouts of a number of Earthlings who'd been implanted with monitoring chips, including Marty.

"We had to tell them all about Buddy and his funeral," Will said. "They'd enjoyed monitoring him for a number of years. That's how they always found the good bars to visit.

They'd wait until Buddy appeared stationary for a number of months and they saw a pattern. When he was immobile, he'd found a bar he liked. They hadn't checked in on him in a number of years when they found he'd spent the past decade in Darwin. They were preparing a big expedition to see the twine ball and the bar Buddy'd made a home. But we told them Buddy was dead and their damn chip was still sending information from his tomb beneath the frozen Minnesota ground."

Orla explained that the chip in Buddy, the one they'd installed when they'd found him drunk in the hedge with fire ants crawling all over his ass, was practically prehistoric. It merely showed location.

"Now, the chip in your butt —"

"Yeah, I'd nearly forgot about that, those one-armed little bastards," Marty said with a red flash of irritation.

"Of course, they put them in us, too. That's what aliens do, you know. But none of that's important. What is important is what we discovered on Gonto. We now have it within our means to become gods. To live forever."

"Take it from me," Marty said, "you don't want to live forever."

"You will when you hear this," Will said. "Jesus is coming back in six weeks. He told us all about it. Paradise is right around the corner."

Marty remembered dy Ego confiding in him that Jesus was planning on returning to Earth in 2081. He remembered doing the nasty math and thinking he'd have to live to be 118 years old to be around. It seemed a ridiculous proposition at the time, one he'd immediately dismissed. But here he was, by God, on the very cusp of that grand old age. In a scant few months Jesus would be here and Marty could fulfill a lifelong ambition and finally meet Him. Then he looked around the room and realized it simply wasn't meant to be.

"There's no way in hell anyone's going to get Jesus Christ to pay $25 to stand in line to gamble on the life of a dying old man," Marty moaned. "Poor Buster here would be put right on the spot, too. What if Jesus came in here and healed all my infirmities? There would be riots in the street. The mob might crucify the poor guy all over again. And I sure won't be able to get up and walk out of here to meet Him."

Will and Orla exchanged conspiratorial grins. "Don't be too sure about that," Orla said.

"Okay, what gives? How'd you do it? You found the fountain of youth. That's what you really found, wasn't it?" Marty said.

"We didn't find it," Orla said. "We created it."

"People for the past 100 years have been going to plastic surgeons to buff and puff, shrink and pinken their skins," Will said. "Orla knew that wasn't the way to go. She figured there had to be a formula. My whole life I've been driven to find the reasons why some of us age more quickly than others. Why are some blessed with longevity and what would it take to seize that trait? Was it the fine red wines they consume near the sunny Mediterranean? The rice staples of our friends in the Orient? Was it aloe? Vitamin E? Gingko biloba? Nope. It was none of those things. Orla?"

She said, "It turns out the common denominator is …"

"Yes?" It was Dudash.

"Hope," Orla said. "The thing that makes us live life is . . . hope. Grandpa and I figured it wasn't something organic that made us live longer, it was hope. Hope that tomorrow will be better. That our arthritic hands won't ache so bad. That the home team won't make the last out. We've all seen it over and over. If the doctor tells the sick patient that a cure is on the way, she gets better. Study after study shows that placebos can work just as effectively as the real things."

"Except when the pills could ensure a euphoric state was reached," Will interjected, reflexively defending mass consumption of drugs. Still, he could not deny that the human emotion of hope was key. "So Orla and I set out on Gonto to make a dose of hope. We sat down and made a list of all the most hopeful things we could think of. And then we set the Gontoians off on a scavenger hunt during their trips to Earth. They made a game out of it. For such a contented people, they can be very competitive."

Orla described how the joyful Gontoians came dashing off their space crafts with armloads of his orders to see who could bring the most hopeful items from Earth, the things that start out fresh with good wishes and the promise of better tomorrows.

"They'd have Christmas wrapping paper, the water from a gardener's hose, the page from a Bible that contains John 3:16, some morning dew from the Latrobe golf course where Arnold Palmer learned to golf. All kinds of things."

"We got mist from the vapors of rainbows," Will said. "Milk from the lips of kittens, tears from an ovulating virgin and sequins from her wedding dress."

Marty, recalling "The Sound of Music" sang out: "These are a few of my favorite things!"

"I admit it sounds foolish," Orla said. "But perhaps the very whimsy of our efforts was what led to success. Well, sort of."

"Sort of?" Marty said.

"We tried it on the most hopeful thing we could think of," Will said. "That being dog pound puppies when they see you walk past their cages. There's nothing more sad or hopeful. Anyone with a heart would want to take the whole bunch home and that's just what we did. The Gontoians cleared the kennels at animal shelters around the country so we could experiment on them. We just mixed it up and poured it in their little bowls. And it worked. Old dogs began to grow young."

"Not only did it work," Orla said, "but it increased the sex drives of these horny dogs — the ones who still had their goodies — and now they've got more horny dogs than they know what to do with."

Marty, recollecting the angry white-haired males, observed to himself how life was a series of tradeoffs.

Will and Orla felt confident enough in their results to risk their lives as human guinea pigs. Gontoians, who already enjoy life spans of 300 years, saw no pressing need to extend their durations. Remember, he said, they are a very contented race. But the tests were failures.

"Understand, Marty, I, like you, was already an old man," Hugh said. "We anticipated that, like the canines, I would begin to feel and appear younger or at least enjoy the recollection of an erection. This did not happen."

"It didn't work for me, either," Orla said. "And I'm talking about the youth part, not the erection."

"You?" Marty asked. "What would a gorgeous young girl like you want to be part of any of these experiments?"

"Marty," Will asked, "how old do you think she is?"

"I'd always guessed around 20," Marty said.

"Marty, Orla is 64."

She smiled and Marty, out of habit, looked to see if his erection was still intact. To his instant chagrin, it had faded.

Will said he had a hunch and sent his alien scavengers on one last hunt.

"We sent them in search of the one magic ingredient we were lacking that is known for giving hope to humans," Will said. "Orla?"

The eyes in the room, even Buster's, turned toward Orla, who was reaching into another zippered pocket in her jump suit. From it she pulled a tiny, silver chunk of metal.

It was a pop tab.

"One of Buddy's pop tabs," Orla said. "We melted these down and stirred mere drops in the concoction and processed them into the pills. It worked! We were young again! If it worked for us, it can work for you."

She removed a small amber pill bottle out of a fourth zippered pocket, fumbled with the tricky child prevention cap and eventually produced a single silver pill that was identical in shape and heft to one of the pop tabs Buddy'd compiled throughout his life. She held it in her palm as it shimmered and danced in the fluorescent ceiling lights. Marty felt the room begin to buzz.

From another zippered pocket, she produced a shot glass and a tiny vial of liquid that looked like quicksilver. "You need to take it with this," Orla said. "It's an instigator."

The word made Marty think of all the times elementary school teachers had called him that very same thing and they had without exception meant troublemaker.

"Dudash?" He summoned her to his bedside to help him up. From the bed he arose for the first time in 18 months. Orla set the pill on the tray beside the glass of ice water. Marty stole a quick glance over at Buster, whose eyes were focusing on the clock above the bed. Less than two minutes remained.

"Now, I have to warn you," Will said. "The transformation will not be without some discomfort. The good news is before that sets in, you're likely to be transported to a time of perfect bliss and contentment. Then there's this … well, let's just stick with discomfort. Then almost instantaneously you're fine. The years will begin to wash off you before our very eyes."

"How much discomfort?" Marty asked.

"A little nausea, slight headache," Will said. "I imagine there have been entire decades when you've woken up feeling worse."

Orla was less evasive, "Oh, you're going to feel like you're going to die. It's gonna hurt like hell."

Will shot Orla a scolding look. "It's a bit unpleasant."

"Oh, no, it's hell, all right," she said.

"But don't forget the bliss and contentment part," Will hastened.

"Yes, there's that, but the rest is absolute hell," she reaffirmed, as if she needed to.

The options were making Marty dizzy and he again thought of game show host Monte Hall. Door No. 1: Bliss, excruciating pain and the youth-restoring potential to live forever. Door No. 2: the hellish purgatory of the status quo.

He reached for the pill. Becky Dudash, as if she were in a dream, reached out to steady the hand, her arm around his size 32 waist. George Prince stood near the foot of the bed too transfixed to even care that the magic pill might cost him nearly $1 billion.

Marty raised the glass to his lips. It smelled to Marty like the sweet, salty tears of nervous virgins. He turned to Will.

"Will? What was yours?"

"My what?"

"Your moment of perfect contentment."

Will's smile betrayed a slight embarrassment that Marty found endearing.

"It was the night we got arrested by old Palley," he said, grinning. "They hauled the four of us in — me, you, Buddy and Skip — and I just remember laughing in the back of that paddy wagon. We'd already made so much money and had so much fun. None of us cared that we'd be going to jail. I was with three guys I loved and I knew then that my life was going to be interesting. I think one of the reasons I was so driven the rest of my life was because I wanted to find that kind of belonging and contentment again. Until Orla came along and expressed an interest in my quests, I never did. I was too concerned with making money. Now, with eternal life in our grasp I feel like I can do something that will let people like me erase those mistakes. I hope so."

Marty's face creased into a grin. He remembered it, too. It had been giggly, ecstatic fun. The pull of that sublime feeling convinced him to roll the dice one more time.

He snatched the pop tab pill off the tray and raised the glass to each of the people in the room. He looked at them with new eyes. In each he saw only humanity and in that he saw only goodness. To immobile Buster, he gave a nod and a wink. Buster even winked back.

"To better days!" he said. "I guess I'm going to get to meet Jesus after all!"

He popped the pill in his mouth and slugged the instigator down in one big gulp.

Dudash was shocked at the immediate effect. McCrae's feet left the ground as the potion delivered its punch to his solar plexus. She held him so tightly they later found controversial black and blue marks handcuffing his wrists.

Marty felt an exhilaration akin to stepping out of an airplane wearing a parachute packed by drunks. With open eyes looking at white walls, he saw only blue. Twilight blue with bits of cloud snagged on the sky flying by like cotton cannonballs. He was fascinated. Where was it taking him?

He'd lived 118 years and had forgotten entire decades. What was the best time of his life? Was it the night in Negril with the three native girls? The day he'd won $20,000 golfing against congressional crooks only to triple it at the blackjack tables? And the squad of showgirls that followed? Good God, he wondered. What if it happened to be family time that he'd squandered throughout life's chase?

He was dying to know.

What he saw made him think the transmission had mistakenly jumped networks. Dudash lightened her grip when she saw him reach out into thin air as if to change an invisible channel.

It was the face of his older brother, Tom. He was holding a balloon in one hand and a pink pillow of cotton candy in the other. He was smiling. No, he was clowning. He was making funny faces that had the appeal and joy of a circus, all on a little boy's loving mug.

Huh?

Marty's head turned in the hospital room and gazed upward at the empty ceiling. It was his mother. She may have looked prettier on her wedding day, but Marty doubted it. She was a vision, young and lovely. Her girlish brown hair glowed in the autumn sunshine. It had to be autumn. The trees in the park were as tartan as a Scotsman's kilt. He was admiring the kindness in the face above him when another leaned in and kissed it.

Dad! He was lean and swaggering. If there were other girls around, they would surely be jealous of Mom, her being with a man so handsome. A halo of smiles hovered above his head. And that's when Marty remembered it. They were going to an amusement park near Pittsburgh. The day was one of perfect happiness. Perfect pleasure. Perfect love. He was 2 and his joy was complete. It wasn't the love he had chased all his life that had mattered. It was the love with which he'd been born, a love that would color the whole rest of his days.

He looked around for Judas, but couldn't find him. He hadn't been born yet. If this was supposed to mean Judas killed the fun for the rest of his life, Marty wasn't buying it. He thought things only got better after Judas came along and no drug-induced dream would ever convince him otherwise. Judas had made everything better.

Still, there could be no denying he'd been in his first euphoric state when he was just 2 years old.

He felt tears streaming down his face. It was the most happy moment of a life filled to busting with joy. The instant that recognition hit home, the second it dawned on him that he'd spent the past 116 years vainly but happily trying to equal that infant moment, that's when it ended. It felt like an angry lumberjack had swung an ax at his forehead. The pain was excruciating. The memory was gone and he was back in the malevolent present.

"Yeeeowww!" he screamed. "Sweet Jesus, my head feels like it's going to explode!"

He tore loose from Dudash's grip and began thrashing about the room. He knocked over the hospital tray and flung both the shot glass to the floor. He ran directly into the prone, saluting Buster and sent him reeling rigidly into the wall.

Years later, Dudash and George would describe it to their children that it was exactly like watching a chicken with its head cut off. Will and Orla looked positively nonplussed by the frantic dance. Orla reached into a fifth zippered pocket and pulled another small shot glass and another beaker. George, Dudash and Buster would later swear in court it was bourbon.

"Marty! Listen to me. You need to drink this! Right now! Drink it! Drink it!" Will said. Marty's eyes were bulging. His mouth was curled as if waiting for a cerebral signal to unleash another scream. His thin, flat, white hair splayed out like each strand was trying to launch itself off the surface of his skull.

"What the hell is it!?" Marty roared.

"It's the antidote to all the killing poison you just swallowed," Will said. "Strong stuff. Now, drink! You can't have one without the other. Or you'll die!"

"We think," Orla said mildly.

Marty's eyes pinballed back and forth between Will and Orla. He felt like dying now. This stuff was killing him and he was in terrific pain. But he remembered he really wanted to see Jesus.

He drank.

Buster, who was slowly beginning to reanimate, was the only one who noticed there were just 40 seconds on the clock. Marty drained the shot in one dousing gulp. He smacked his lips, swiped a robed forearm across his mouth and began to smile broadly. The beatific smile seemed to wash years off his face and for a moment he appeared majestic, immortal.

He drew one deep, last breath and said in a clarion voice that reverberated down the halls like Gabriel's horn, "That which does not kill me, can only make me stronger!"

He stood stock still for three full seconds, his right fist raised in euphoric salute. They all watched as his buckeye brown eyes rolled back in his head, and his frail, old body slowly crumpled into a heap on the faded linoleum. His soul squirted straight out of his body and went directly to Dreamville where Buddy was smiling sunshine and waiting to boost him unto an old donkey. Both Buddy and the burro were wearing sombreros.

Marty was dead before he hit the floor.

There were eight ticks left on the clock.

Orla flicked her brunette hair back behind her right ear, looked at Will and said, "Well, that's peculiar. You know, I always imagined he was the kind of guy who was sure to die laughing."

"Let's get the hell out of here!" Will said. He shoved George out of the way, pulled the lever and disappeared down the chute.

Oral stroked her chin, smiled at George and Becky and said, "Oh, well. Back to the drawing board!" And then she was gone.

Buster, Dudash and George all stood transfixed over the final remains of Marty McCrae. Buster reached down and felt for a pulse he knew was not there.

He stood up, looked at Dudash, shrugged and said, "We have a winner! … I guess."

Chris Rodell

He reached into his pants pocket and started cursing the ancient lighter he'd stolen from his grandfather back when he was just a boy.

It was over.

Out in the hall, on the wrong side of the doors, stood Marshal Marshall Palley III who became an instant trivia question as the man who was just seconds away from having it all.

Edwards Brothers Malloy
Thorofare, NJ USA
January 13, 2016